·G·E·N·N·I·E·

The Huguenot Woman

BY Bette M. Ross:

Song of Deborah
Gennie, the Huguenot Woman

·G·E·N·N·I·E·

The Huguenot Woman

Bette M. Ross

Fleming H. Revell Company
Old Tappan, New Jersey

Library of Congress Cataloging in Publication Data

Ross, Bette M.
  Gennie, the Huguenot woman

  1. Huguenots—History—Fiction.   I. Title.
PS3568.O842H8   1983   813'54   82-24128
ISBN 0-8007-1358-3

TO my mother,
who told me
the best picture is still unpainted,
the best book is still unwritten

·F·O·R·E·W·O·R·D·

he word *Huguenot* comes from the German and means "sworn companion." It is the name given to French Protestants of the seventeenth and eighteenth centuries.

In those dangerous years, they were among France's most respected citizens—skilled craftspersons, artisans, and countrymen whose farms and dairies bloomed with the fruit of their diligence.

Inevitably their wealth and success attracted the envy of elements of the Catholic monarchy. Under the banner of religious heresy, a succession of French kings killed or enslaved thousands of Huguenot families and seized their holdings.

While Huguenots were enduring persecution in France, Protestants from other nations were forging peaceable lives in the New England colonies, coexisting with Catholic French Canada.

These New Englanders shook their heads over the shortsightedness of France, which would admit only Catholics into Canada and yet badly needed more settlers. Why could not the Catholics be more like them?

The Protestants conveniently forgot the heroism and courage of past generations of French Catholic priests who endured deprivation, pain, and often death at the hands of Indian nations to whom they brought the gospel.

Nor did these New World Protestants like to be reminded of their own bloody background, when the Salem witch trials proved that anyone at all can most basely use religion to justify his secret desires.

·G·E·N·N·I·E·

The Huguenot Woman

he tensed as his rough hand settled lightly on her shoulder. It slipped to the shallow of her waist. They were lying spoon fashion, their bodies not otherwise touching. His fingers caressed her warm back before his hand slid up to her shoulder and played with her ear lobe.

He must have felt her tautness then, for he stopped. "What is the matter?"

"Your brother. Why did he come here yesterday?"

Flourinot expelled a breath of exasperation and fell back. "You never let a thing go."

Marie Therese turned toward him. "He frightens me so I can hardly breathe."

"Now Georges frightens you. I don't know what is the matter with you lately."

How could he be so blind? she thought. This time Georges had two others with him, dressed in the king's livery. How shameful it was that Flourinot—his own brother!—had had to stand by like a field peasant while Georges and the soldiers thumped over the Harmonie's neat farm, the men's heavy boots leaving clots of earth on Marie Therese's freshly swept brick floor. Did they think the Harmonies were sheltering spies, for heaven's sake? Their family was as loyal as any to Louis!

Her hand caressed her husband's hard chest in a placating gesture. "Oh, Flourinot, if he were like you, I wouldn't be so frightened. He's so, so—"

"Catholic."

He couldn't see her worried smile in the predawn. She and Flourinot had first met in a little French Protestant church, where seventeen years ago they had been married. Protestants—Huguenots, they called themselves—were seldom bothered in those days. But recently the Catholics had stirred up the king's hatred against them. Georges' branch of the family was adamantly Catholic.

As if he could read her mind, Flourinot said, "Do not worry, *ma petite chou*; Georges is family. A strong Catholic family member is good protection. It is good to know someone in power." His deep voice rumbled with confidence.

After a while she said, "I love you." He turned back to her. Their hands explored the familiar terrain of each other's bodies, and Marie Therese gladly abandoned her fears to the fires of their pleasure.

Gennie Harmonie glanced at her parents' closed door. It must be earlier than she thought. She rose from her pallet at one side of the stone hearth and padded across to the door leading outside. A long slant of rose gold widened on the cold bricks under her feet as she opened it. A cock crowed. She glanced again at her parents' door, puzzled. Why were they still abed?

She stretched and yawned deeply, moved her hands across her ribs and then up over her breasts. Her small, full lips broke into a smile of contentment with herself and the new day. Gennie's face was heart shaped, with softly rounded cheeks and a delicately pointed chin. Her father had once likened her eyes to a trout pond. When she had pounced on him in protest, he had insisted it was so: They were warm and flecked, a deep, still brown, full of promise.

She glanced back into the room. Phillippe was still asleep, too, lazy boy, on the other side of the hearth. His rosy lips were parted, his lashes, like hers, a thick fringe, now resting on his downy cheeks. At eight, Phillippe played harder, ate more, and slept more soundly than any of them. Gennie smiled at him as she began to dress, quickly in the chilly air, and noiselessly.

Pulling on her undergarments before she shed her nightgown, on which she had embroidered sky blue loveknots, Gennie struggled into her everyday dress. The waist hiked uncomfortably around her ribs, felt too tight across her chest, and she felt, exposed far too much of her ankles. She had spurted nearly a handspan since her sixteenth birthday, when the dress had been new.

As she combed her thick hair and tied a kerchief round it, her gaze strayed out the doorway, past the kitchen garden and the apple orchard. She could not see the wheat field, hidden as it was by the thorny hedge of gooseberry bushes that kept the goats out of the garden, but golden-topped mounds of harvested wheat poked above the hedge here and there. She headed for the well.

The Harmonie farm was not far from the port of Le Havre, on the Normandy coast. It was fed by little branchlets of the River Seine that wound like pig tails through the lush farmlands. From the highest point of their farm could be seen the tiny specks in the harbor at Le Havre, which were the tips of tall sailing ships. On such a ship, her cousin Etienne had sailed away.

The morning was so beautiful that Gennie was seized with a desire to see the ships once again. Wouldn't it be wonderful if Etienne were on one of them right now, coming home! She set down the bucket of water she had just drawn and set off for the hillock.

In the distance she could make out a party on horseback, coming her way. A vague feeling of alarm sprang within her breast. Their farm lay at the end of the road. Strangers seldom came this way.

Now she could see that all but one were in blue and white—the king's livery. And the other, the leader, was clad loosely in a black robe.

Gennie let out a little gasp of fear. She picked up her skirts and raced for the cottage, screaming for her parents as she went.

"Papa! Papa, Mama! A Black Robe is coming—and soldiers!" She burst through the door. "Phillippe, honey, get up. Get dressed!" She shook him roughly as she flew by and barged into her parents' room.

Flourinot was already dressed. Marie Therese sat up, clutching the bedclothes, as she entered. "Gennie, how many times—"

"The soldiers are back." Her voice teetered on the edge of panic. "A Black Robe is leading them."

"Oh, Flourinot . . ." Marie Therese hesitated only a moment. Then she was out of bed and reaching for her clothing. "Is Georges with them?"

"I didn't see him. I don't think so."

"Get Phillippe," said her father. "You two stay here with your mother, while I talk to them."

"Papa, I want to—"

"Do as you're told!"

Phillippe had already run into the bedroom, to the safety of his mother's plump arms.

Flourinot cast about as if seeking a weapon.

Suddenly Gennie heard horses racing into the yard. It sounded as if they were coming right into the cottage.

"Come out, Flourinot Harmonie, by order of the king! Your family, too! Everyone, outside!"

A soldier sprang down, a sabre rattling at his side. A black-robed Jesuit priest leaned down and handed him a scroll. Without once glancing at the astonished Flourinot, he read: "By order of Louis the Fifteenth, by grace of God king and absolute monarch. To make France pure in the sight of God and His Holiness, Pope Benedict the Fourteenth, God's emissary on earth, be it declared that all pagans be uprooted and flung from this land. In his mercy, Louis has invited those who would to recant. Failing this most Christian duty, he is sorrowfully forced to purge the faithless from God's holy soil . . . ."

Behind her husband, Marie Therese stuffed her apron to her mouth. "Flourinot, Flourinot, what is he saying?"

Now two more soldiers dismounted. One lit a torch from his flint box. At the sight of the torch leaping into flame, Gennie screamed and flung her arms around Phillippe. Now they were being pulled roughly outside. Other torches were lit. Soldiers dashed inside. Two disappeared around back and one headed on horseback toward the haymows.

Flourinot ran from one to the other, trying to stop them. They pushed him roughly away but did not harm him. Finally he ran to the priest and clutched at the sandaled foot in the stirrup.

"Why? Why?"

The priest looked down coldly. "We are making an example of your family, Harmonie. Others will not be so foolhardy as to deny God, when they see the cost."

"We do not deny God! God, help us! What will you do with us?"

"That, too, has been decided."

Suddenly soldiers seized Gennie and Phillippe and wrenched them apart. Each was hustled up behind a remounting soldier. Gennie saw Marie Therese's hands being bound before her. Hands in gauntlets lifted her mother in front of a horseman.

"You leave my mother alone!"

"It will be all right, Gennie." Marie Therese's face was rigid with fear. "Georges will help us. Your father will get word to Georges."

Gennie's father had been trussed like a goose and flung over their own mule. Flames spurted from the window and door of their cottage and licked at the edges of the sod roof. Around them, the haymows were bursting into fireballs.

The leader glanced around swiftly. "That will do it."

Teeth chattering in fear, Gennie clung to the hard waist of the rider as the horse leaped forward.

———————————— ◆ ————————————

By noon, the procession was clattering through the cobbled streets of Le Havre. The odors of the city sewers rose to greet them in the humid summer air.

"Hold them here."

The sun blazed on the high, whitewashed walls of the Ursuline convent. A few meters away, in the center of the street, the leader dismounted and ordered passersby to raise the heavy iron cover that led down into the city's sewers.

"God have mercy, God have mercy," shrieked Marie Therese at the sight.

Why was her mother so frightened? So far they had not been harmed. Perhaps now they were to be let go, after such a terrible warning. Yes, they were being helped down.

The Jesuit's fingers bit into Gennie's upper arm as he pushed the women toward a small wooden door near one corner of the convent wall. Gennie glanced around. Papa and Phillippe were still in the center of the street. She struggled. The priest's strong fingers drove into her flesh.

Suddenly Phillippe screamed. Gennie twisted around to see the soldiers pitch her father head first down the sewer. Phillippe was struggling in the grasp of another man at the edge of the black hole.

"Oh, no. Oh, no!" she screamed. "Phillippe! Phillippe!" Somehow she tore away from the priest as her brother was dropped into the sewer after her father. "Help! Somebody do something!"

Gennie dashed toward the hole. The peasants and burghers of Le Havre pressed silently against the walls and shop stalls. No one lifted a hand to stop the king's soldiers.

"Fetch that girl!" the priest commanded.

Gennie dropped to the cobblestones and hung over the sewer. "Papa! Phillippe!"

"Gennie," Phillippe's voice quavered. "I'm scared. It's dark down here."

"D-don't be scared, Phillippe. Our Savior is with us," sobbed Gennie.

She felt herself being pulled to her feet. They dragged her back to the convent.

"You can thank your pagan God you're alive at all," the soldier muttered as he thrust her through the gate.

·C·H·A·P·T·E·R·2·

or three days Gennie fancied she could hear Phillippe's cries.

Within the high walls of the convent, they were not further confined. Daily mother and daughter crouched before the solid door, in the corner of the wall, leading to the street. Did anyone hear their cries for someone to rescue Phillippe and Flourinot?

The silent sisters did not meet their eyes. With strong, certain gestures they met their bodily needs: Here is your cell, your blanket. There the chamber pot, this way to the refectory.

But who can eat or sleep knowing that loved ones are suffering? surely not meant to die! Nightly mother and daughter clung together and repeated their prayers.

"We must not give up hope," Marie Therese gasped the third night, as if trying to control her own breathless fear. Her dark, worried eyes avoided Gennie's. "Our dear Jesus tells us we must ask and then conduct ourselves in the belief that he has heard us."

Gennie did not care. She would believe anything, do anything she was told, if only Phillippe could be once again teasing and laughing with her, if only her dear papa . . . Turning away from her mother, she sobbed into the pallet.

Marie Therese's fingers stroked the damp mass of hair away from her fevered temples. "We must also be thankful that we have been spared, Gennie," she said in a quieter voice. We must put ourselves in God's hands and follow where he leads."

"But why, Mama, why did this happen?" She felt her mother's head shaking against hers. After a moment Marie Therese hugged her. "Go to sleep, precious one."

Sister Margarethe strode across the yard, her full, black skirts flapping. Beneath the huge, starched cowl, her plain features were composed, though shiny with perspiration—from the heavy wool habit as much as from the heat of the day. As Gennie and Marie Therese watched, the nun made directly for them.

They had been at the Ursuline convent two weeks. In that time no one had addressed them or in any way acknowledged their presence, save by necessity. Both rose as Sister Margarethe approached.

"Madame Harmonie. Gennie." The nun's voice was low and pleasant, her eyes windows to a kindly nature. "I am Sister Margarethe. We have not been unaware of your suffering. Had it been in our power to help you, we surely would have done so. Will you walk with me?"

Gennie snatched her mother's hand as they adjusted their steps to the nun's measured tread. Marie Therese was a little shorter than her daughter, with the full, healthy figure of a farm wife. Her brown eyes, so like Gennie's, were ringed with shadow.

"It is our understanding that you are to be kept here for the rest of your lives."

Gennie caught her breath. Marie Therese's hand squeezed hers, warning her to be silent. Sister Margarethe appeared not to notice.

"Willingly, we here serve our Lord Jesus Christ. It is disturbing to our harmony to know that our sisters are being detained against their wills." She paused and considered them. "For we all are sisters, are we not?"

Marie Therese said, "I never thought of . . ." Her voice trailed off, and she nodded.

"Yes." Sister Margarethe walked on. "I have been instructed to offer you an alternative. There are French Protestant families living in the English colonies in the New World. We have always known that their homes are open to receive those who are disaffected with—with King Louis's reign. Shall I continue?"

"No!" Gennie burst out. "Mama, we can't leave Papa and Phillippe. We have to stay here!"

"Gennie, heart. Etienne is in the New World, remember."

Gennie had not seen her handsome, dashing cousin for years, but she remembered well his dark, swarthy good looks, his confident swagger around their kitchen as he spun tales of other men who had sailed to New France and returned with fortunes. But Etienne had never returned. Was he still there, still a coureur de bois, trapping and selling furs and becoming rich?

In the silence, Marie Therese said to the nun, "Please go on, Sister Margarethe."

"If you will consent to become bondservants for seven years, your passage will be paid, and your lodging and sustenance will be guaranteed during your servitude. After that time, you will be free." She paused, then added, "And it is my understanding that in the English colonies you will be free to worship our Lord in your own manner."

"Is this possible? How can you . . . ? I have heard that French ships are forbidden to sail into English colonies, as the English are forbidden to visit New France. Merciful God, is it a trick?"

"Madame Harmonie, please!" They had reached the end of the courtyard. Sister Margarethe turned about and faced them. "We are thinking only of you. One of our pleasant tasks here is to prepare young Frenchwomen of sound breeding to become wives and mothers in New France. We teach the girls sewing and cooking, something of gardening and herbs, healing skills, and spinning and weaving.

"The authorities pay scant attention when our girls leave the convent en masse to prepare for their journey. Should you go, you would take your places in their class, but when they are placed on a French sailing ship, you and your daughter would be—ah—misplaced and sent to England." Sister Margarethe's lips parted in a sudden, conspiratorial smile that took years from her countenance.

"I believe the English experience a similar difficulty in obtaining females to bear their next generation in the colonies. It is my firm belief that you will be well received and well regarded."

The nun drew a book from her ample sleeve. It was slightly larger than her palm, bound in supple calfskin. "Gennie, dear child, this is for you. Line the pages carefully, so that your hand may not develop careless penmanship. This we give to all our girls. Examine your behavior every day, to keep your mind stayed upon our Savior. Seek his will in all you do. A quill and ink is in your cell."

Gennie curtsied, as she had been taught. "Thank you, Sister."

The nun nodded. "Then I shall leave you to consider your decision. If you choose to act, the letters, including your consent to servitude, will be sent tomorrow. You will leave two weeks following." With a brisk smile, she left them.

"Wait!" Marie Therese hurried after the nun. "Sister, we do thank you for your kindness. But, please, have you any word of my husband and my little boy?"

Gennie clasped her hands and hugged them under her chin.

Sister Margarethe flicked a glance at her before answering her mother. "I wish you had not asked. I can tell you nothing good. They are in all probability dead. Remember them in your prayers, but do not torment yourself with believing that you will see them again in this life." She hesitated, then added, "Madame, I urge you to leave France!"

Gennie's face went white. She clutched her mother's arm. "Our blessed Savior would not let them die! We must stay right here, Mama!"

Tears coursed down Marie Therese's face. Her shoulders sagged as if she no longer had strength to hold back the nightmare of the past weeks. She appeared not to have heard Gennie's frightened voice. As if to herself, she said, "Yes. We must believe that our dear Lord has heard our prayers ... that he is guiding our steps ... Sister Margarethe? If we go to the New World, my daughter and I must not be separated."

"That may be stipulated."

"*Eh, bien.* We will go."

"Mama! How will they find us?"

Marie Therese raised hopeless eyes to Sister Margarethe.

The nun's eyes filled with compassion. To Gennie she said, "We will tell them where you have been sent." She lifted her fingers toward her lips in a benedictory farewell.

homas Roebuck slipped his hand in the icy water and hauled out his trap. Extricating the heavy beaver carcass, he tossed it up on a snowy bank. With numbed fingers he reset the trap and replaced it in the stream.

Getting to his feet, he thrust his hands into the fur mittens looped around his neck and danced up and down lightly, his breath making little cloud puffs. He squinted at the sun. Still early afternoon.

He had left home nine days ago, to check the trap lines he and his father had set last fall. So far, the harvest was to the good, yielding thick, uniform furs. Thomas considered heading for home. Or he could cache his furs here and harvest the rest of the line. Then he could go back and fetch Pa's horse and carry them all in at once.

His fingers began to tingle with returning circulation. Slipping them out of the mittens, he bent contentedly to the task of skinning the beaver.

Thomas had left his father's farm in a state of irritable restlessness. A storm had sealed them all in the house for weeks, and by early March he had been feeling like a chained bear.

"I swear the older you get the worse you get," complained his mother. "Mr. Roebuck, Thomas has been tormenting the wee ones for nigh on a week. What is to be done w' him?"

William Roebuck understood his son's restlessness. Their energetic natures chafed at the long winter months' confinement. While their Quaker neighbors closer in to Philadelphia contented themselves with carving furniture and decorating lintel and post with painted tulips and roses, men like the Roebucks dismissed this sedentary life as a form of laziness.

Like the Roebucks, nearly all the Scotch-Irish farmers who migrated to mid-eastern Pennsylvania ran traps in winter. Thomas had tended trap lines with his father since he was ten, seven years ago.

Now, to his delight, his father gave in to his mother's pleas and sent him out alone to check their lines. If the weather had been fine, one of his little brothers would have come along, too. But on this trip Thomas was relieved by the solitude, exhilarated by the crystal frost of the air and the headiness of being on his own.

Truth be told, William had planned to come along himself, but then one of the little ones had taken ill; the father reluctantly decided he must remain home, with the horse, should it become necessary to fetch the doctor from Germantown. Until last year, the closest doctor had practiced in Philadelphia. Germantown, only eight miles away, cut the distance in half.

That had left Thomas free to take the pack mule and escape. Of middling height, Thomas had unruly black hair and flashing blue eyes. His impulsiveness, his boundless energies, set him apart from staider citizens. His hair was coarse and inclined to curl. Each morning at home he braided his queue and tied it securely before slicking back the sides with water, then jamming on his tricorn to hold it in place.

Now, as he finished skinning the animal and threw the carcass back in the woods, he thought of the cramped, dark cabin, reeking with odors from a continual fire, cooked cabbage and potatoes, and bodies encased in half a dozen layers of linsey-woolsey. Thomas grinned in guilty acknowledgment. Go back before he absolutely must? Of course he would go on and finish the whole line!

"What is so funny, *mon ami?*"

Thomas whirled and gripped his knife.

"Oh, no, no, no, it is only Captain Jack." Stepping out of the trees not a dozen yards away was a woodsman dressed similarly to himself, as dark as a Spaniard and speaking a gumbo of French and English. A pack of furs, smaller than Thomas's, was strapped to his back.

He watched the man forge through the snowpack. He saw the man's eyes drift over his own pack.

"You been out long time?"

"No. You?" Thomas rapidly assessed the other. Feet encased in large pieces of buckskin bound up around the calves. A pair of rabbits dangling from the belt of a grease-stained parka. The man had watchful black eyes and a heavy beard, which now bristled with icicles. Thomas straddled his pack and folded his arms, hoping he looked able to take care of himself. The man was maybe eight or ten years older and looked fit. Thomas was confident he was the stronger of the two.

The dark man watched him intently. Suddenly he said, "Eh!" and stripped off his pack. "I could use a little fire and a drink, *mon ami.* You, too?" He took a pull from his flask and passed it.

Thomas hesitated. In his family drink was only for the sickly.

"Best brandy ever made."

Thomas accepted the flask, and Captain Jack turned his back and set off gathering wood. Thomas sniffed at the flask. It didn't smell quite like what his father kept in the square brown bottle. It was fruitier: more like peach cider. Encouraged, he took a sip.

"Good, heh? Take some more!" Captain Jack dumped his load of kindling beside a fallen log in the clearing and went off to drag in a section of rotting timber.

Thomas took a deep draught of the brandy. This time it flowed like hot syrup into his stomach. His eyes watered. "It sure does warm a body!" declared Thomas. He set the flask aside and kindled the fire.

The two men settled on their packs and passed the brandy back and forth. Captain Jack had a way of watching Thomas without seeming to. Came from a lifetime of stalking animals, Thomas told himself. Well, he would just put the man at his ease.

"Where you from?"

Captain Jack had come from Trois-Rivières, he told Thomas, fabled Canadian home of coureurs de bois for over a century. His mother was Huron, his father a blackamoor from the West Indies. And his grandmother on his mother's side was a spirit-god. They communicated with her in dreams from the nether world of the manitous.

His lips parted, Thomas listened and watched in fascination. He'd never heard of manitous, who, it seemed, were Indian spirits who lived all about them, in the woods and the streams. Even the echo was a manitou who must be appeased, if provoked from his slumber.

The sun sharpened the landscape with long needles of shadow. As he talked, Captain Jack untied his rabbits and skinned and gutted them while Thomas sharpened a green branch and fashioned a brace over the fire. His head throbbed now, and once in a while he saw two of Captain Jack.

They devoured the rabbit meat, Thomas not forgetting a muttered "Thank 'e Lord" before tearing at the charred flesh, washing it down with brandy swilled like ale. The meat tasted better than anything he had ever eaten, and he felt himself bolder and stronger than ever before. He gazed at his new friend, thinking how good life was.

Eventually they settled down in their sleeping robes, feet toward the banked fire, and he listened to Captain Jack's voice resonating through the night. Overhead, the stars glittered like a swarm of fireflies tangled in a silver braid. Thomas smiled contentedly. How good life was!

e dim-witted, stupid lad! Is this how I've raised ye? To let a half-breed do ye out of a winter's worth of furs? *Here* is the new goods for your brothers' trousers!" *Whap.* "Here is the new traps!" *Whap.* "And *here* is the musket ye been jawing on about!" *Whap.* "If that iniquitous knave had took me mule, I'd a' turned ye over to the parson for a public whipping."

Thomas raised his arms to fend off the worst of the blows that his father rained on his head and shoulders. It never occurred to him to resist. He knew they were deserved.

With sickness in his head and in his stomach, as helpless as a babe for a whole day after discovering Captain Jack's treachery, Thomas had set off in pursuit the following day. The villain had twenty-four hours on him at least, and light snow had erased the hard edges of his tracks.

The thief had stolen only the furs. By a miraculous gift from Providence, he had failed to discover the mule tethered close at hand. The fourth day of the chase, with a new storm threatening, Thomas was forced to abandon the search. He had expended his food stores and squandered the days allotted for servicing the rest of the line. He had no choice but to return home and submit to his father's wrath.

Now they sat together on the diminished pile of split logs outside the cabin, Roebuck heaving his anger away and Thomas's shoulders smarting. Roebuck grimaced at his son. His ire lessened as he recognized his son's penitence. Life's lessons were hard, to be sure.

"I'll go back out and clear the rest of the line and reset the traps and then check the first half again. It's been a heavy winter."

"Ye'll chop more wood for yer mother first."

"Yes, Pa . . . Anything else?"

"Yer brothers can tend to the rest."

In an awkward attempt at affection, his father wrestled his shoulder. The lad could do with some seasoning, he reckoned as he left Thomas to work out his guilt on the woodpile and went inside.

Before William Roebuck had come to Pennsylvania, he had had his share of misadventure himself, in Ireland, struggling against Catholics who hated the Presbyterians. Pennsylvania had been a haven of green peace. Hailing from the days of William Penn's wise and just treaties with the Indians of his province, no one disturbed the peaceful pursuit of godly pleasures that they knew in Pennsylvania. But Roebuck had heard disturbing news on his last visit to Philadelphia.

The endless rivalry between England and France had exploded in open warfare. Inevitably its tentacles reached the French and English colonies in the New World. French sailing vessels based at Quebec had begun to harass the Grand Banks, capturing English fishing vessels and stealing their catches, abandoning the crews on remote islands where they would be rescued, but none too quickly.

Urgent letters had been sent homeward to England, begging King George for warships to back up the few regiments of disciplined British soldiers and the colonial volunteers. The four colonies of New York, Massachusetts, Connecticut, and New Hampshire together mustered 4,500 recruits. Provincial assemblies in Pennsylvania and the remaining colonies, being farther removed from the French threat, refused to vote any monies to support the war. Owing to the years of peace Pennsylvania had enjoyed, few farmers even owned weapons.

In the tavern used for town meetings in Philadelphia, William Roebuck had listened to those who wanted to recruit a regiment to join the northern colonies. Benjamin Franklin, a talkative and civic-minded printer, led another faction who opposed joining the fray.

Such peace-loving heads had prevailed, and Pennsylvania turned down her sister colonies' pleas.

Interrupting Roebuck's thoughts, Thomas barged in the door and made a beeline for his father. "Pa, I was thinking—after I tend to the lines, of course—I might go farther west, see what's out there." Thomas didn't look at his father, but kept his face resolutely ahead.

Roebuck studied his son's profile. He had a good, strong chin and a small, almost pug nose that gave him an innocent, boyish look that Roebuck suspected would never desert him. He felt a grudging welling of pride in his oldest son, whose spirit seemed at times so far ahead of his reason.

Capable hands shot out of sleeves that only a few months ago had covered the sinewy wrists, but now lacked well over an inch. His woolen trousers lacked even more of reaching his shoe tops. True, Thomas was impulsive, rash, and unthinking on occasion, but he could also be gentle. That he was still bristling with restlessness did not surprise William. He was, after all, seventeen—a man, able to vote and pay taxes and, William realized, eligible to join the militia. He felt a pang at the thought of Thomas moving west, leaving his home forever, sending down new roots, forming new allegiances in alien soil. So unready! Never had to defend himself, never been exposed to . . . "Thomas."

"Yes, Pa?"

"What would ye think about lending a hand in the fight against the French?"

"I thought the gentlemen in Philadelphia voted to stay out of it."

"Aye. But many of the lads are planning to volunteer anyway and join regiments elsewhere."

"By thunder, Pa, that's a fine idea!" A light broke over the youthful features. Then it disappeared.

Roebuck smiled inwardly. His son's emotions were plainest on his face. A horse trader he'd never be, till he learned to keep his countenance. They would trade a few shots, run a few forays, and come home. And Thomas would be rid of the restlessness and ready to settle down. Here, not "out west" somewhere. "What bothers ye, son?"

"The furs. I can't take your musket, and I've nothing to fight with, and now no furs to trade for a piece." An angry flush heated his face. "If I ever catch that thieving poltroon—".

"If not you, someone else: Providence will run him to ground. Perchance there will be enough in the traps after all. I'll ask Mrs. Roebuck to get ye up a food packet."

"Don't worry, Pa. This time I will do it right."

⸺◆⸺

Thomas paused on the crown of a hill on the outskirts of Germantown and gazed down at a sprinkling of farm buildings partially muffled by snow. Here and there black, wet patches mottled the frozen earth, like ragged holes in a quilt. Tassels of trees flagged a cloistered ribbon of stream and stitched up the windward side of the land.

He passed corrals, stone outbuildings, and wooden sheds that were in good repair. Robust smoke billowed gaily from the chimney of the home of mortared stone nestled at the hub of the farm.

Its owner, Henri Zellaire, and his family had migrated here from the Rhine Valley in France in 1735, ten years ago. They were Huguenots, that strange breed of Protestants who had opposed so heroically the most powerful heads of state and church in Europe and gotten themselves butchered or dispossessed for their zeal. Thomas knew that not all the American colonies were easy on people who wanted to worship God in different ways. But in Penn's colony, why, even the Indians could dance and howl about their Great Spirits, and none would say them nay.

Zellaire had never seemed noticeably different to Thomas. A peaceable, energetic, and shrewd man, who had had the misfortune to lose his wife to influenza three winters ago, Zellaire earned a good living as a metal- and gunsmith. In his workshop, adjacent to the house, he carved stocks and fashioned iron pieces and balls for guns.

Thomas dug his elbows into his backpack, to shift the weight of the load. *Ought to be enough furs there to buy a fine piece,* he told himself, *and plenty for ammunition, too.*

His journey into the Appalachian hills, to strip and reset the traps, had netted sufficient furs to pay for necessities for his mother and little brothers, as well as provision him for the militia.

His father had cautioned him to exchange the furs for coin at the earliest opportunity and to carry his money concealed next to his skin. Thomas had felt a little chagrined that his father had felt it necessary to remind him. But the stinging memory of the traps bade him hold his tongue and accept the caution with good grace (and with the painful knowledge that his father was quick to cuff and slow to repent).

As he approached the solid oak door of Zellaire's farmhouse, Thomas heard an unexpected peal of feminine laughter. It didn't sound like any of the Zellaires.

·C·H·A·P·T·E·R·5·

ittle Jean Zellaire opened the door. Thomas walked in and stopped cold. A tiny, chestnut-haired woman bustled about, braiding one child's hair, pausing to button a shirt for another, at the same time chattering rapidly in French at a younger woman, hardly more than a child herself.

Thomas knew enough French to gather that she was instructing the girl about spinning the wool that a third youngster was gravely carding. The child pulled soft puffs of wool off the spiked cards and handed them to the young woman, to be spun into the soft skein fattening around the spindle.

The spinner seemed intent upon her task. Her lips were set in a pout of concentration. Thomas wished she would look up. Her piquant face beneath the massed chestnut hair and the prim round cap intrigued him.

As if divining his thoughts, Gennie suddenly looked at him. Her dark eyes seemed enormous. Her lips were full, yet dainty, in good proportion to the small, determined chin. Her childlike face also held an elusive expression of world-weariness.

The older woman shot a volley of words at Henri Zellaire, who had just come in the door from his workroom. Zellaire threw his hands in the air.

"They are learning English, but when Madame Harmonie realized I am French, she suddenly forgot all her English. Sit, sit, young Thomas. How is your family? You will stay for dinner, *n'est-ce pas?*" Zellaire directed one of his children to pour them some ale.

Suddenly Thomas was seized with awkwardness. He banged his knee against the bench, in the act of pulling it away from the table. He threw a glance toward the spinner to see if she had noticed. While he was watching her, Zellaire's ten-year-old daughter set a wooden tankard of ale at his elbow, which he promptly knocked over when he sat. The brew frothed over the table and trickled into his lap. Up he leaped again, toppling the bench and nearly tilting Zellaire's cup past preserving.

"*Mon dieu,* what is wrong with you today?" said Zellaire.

"I'm sorry, Mr. Zellaire!" Thomas eyed the front of his clothing with embarrassment. He threw another glance at the young woman.

29

How could she help noticing? He thought he detected a twitch at the corners of her mouth, but on she went, demurely spinning.

Zellaire glanced at Gennie, then back at Thomas. "Ah," he said in a broad Gallic tone. "Monsieur Thomas Roebuck, may I present Madame Flourinot Harmonie?"

Marie Therese, finishing the child's hair braid, threw him a warm, quick smile.

"And her daughter, Gennie. Gennie, *fille*, come over here and meet our neighbor."

Obediently Gennie rose and approached the table. Thomas caught a glimpse of trim ankle as her fine-boned hands lifted out her skirt in a curtsy. Her waist seemed only a handspan wide, but maybe that was because the swelling above her waist. . . . Thomas colored, on dangerous ground in his imagination.

Gennie's eyes remained modestly downcast.

"Gen-nie," teased Zellaire.

Gennie lifted her gaze slowly to meet Thomas's. Her expression was solemn as a child's.

He wanted her to talk to him. *"Comment allez vous?"* he managed to get out.

"Very well, thank you," she responded in schoolroom English. Her voice was cool and restrained, but her eyes glinted with the first hint of teasing.

Something, somewhere in the vicinity of his midriff, rebounded like a spring. "That's good! That's good, isn't it, Mr. Zellaire?"

"Oh *merveilleux*," said Zellaire, rolling his eyes. Perhaps fearing that Roebuck was in danger of forgetting why he came, Zellaire added briskly, "All right, Gennie, go on, shoo, back to your spinning."

Gennie's lustrous gaze held Thomas's in a look of shy appraisal. A smile that began in her eyes broke over her features.

That spring went off again in his midriff. He'd give anything to know her thoughts!

Casting a final glance over her shoulder, Gennie slipped back to her place.

"Well, young Master Roebuck, what can I do for you today?"

"Um, ah, what you can do." Thomas concentrated on his red-haired neighbor, the sunburned, freckled face and the watery blue eyes. "I need a musket. I brought some furs. They are by the door. You can take what you think is fair."

"Good. How soon do you need it?"

"Well, er, right away. I am on my way now to join the Connecticut regiment. We are going to fight the French. We are at war, you know. Aren't you going to volunteer, Mr. Zellaire?" Suddenly Thomas sucked in his breath. "Oh, I guess not. Not with all these children. And you being French . . ." His face took on the look of one with a toothache.

Zellaire nodded impatiently. "I understand. You fight the Papists. Serves them right. They deserve to lose Canada, since they will not admit good French blood of other faiths." Henri Zellaire poked a finger at Thomas's chest. "Mark me, Thomas Roebuck, the colonies would be much better off if the French and English kings fought each other across the channel and left us alone!

"It would give them less time to meddle in our business," he muttered under his breath.

Thomas nodded courteously. Privately he did not agree. He could hardly wait to join the regiment. He could hear the marching feet . . .

"No, I do not like war," Zellaire was saying. "Like our neighbors the Moravians and the Quakers, heh?" While he spoke, Zellaire led the way through the spacious room into his workshop. Several unfinished walnut stocks were propped against one wall, along with three or four long, metal barrels. On a table, a large, flat trencher held a variety of small, hand-fashioned parts.

Ignoring these, Zellaire unwrapped a long rifle and cradled it like a mother admiring a new baby. "Isn't she beautiful?" Lustily he kissed the burnished stock, then vigorously wiped the spot with an oiled rag. "A flint-lock, I call it. It will give you twice the distance of one of his majesty's muskets."

"*Two* hundred yards?" Thomas watched closely while Henri loaded. "Takes a time to load, doesn't it?"

Henri nodded. "But you'll never need a second shot. Once you bring down a deer with this, you will never want to use a musket again!"

Thomas hefted the piece, frowning. He wished his father were here. He did not yet trust his own judgment.

Henri leaned in. "I use a bullet slightly smaller than the bore. If you wrap it in a patch of well-greased cloth, she'll load faster. And the patch keeps gas from escaping around the bullet, so you achieve more force. We should go out and try it, *n'est-ce pas?*"

Thomas held the rifle aloft. "Yes," he said reverently.

ennie's eyes followed Thomas's muscular figure as the two men trooped back through the house and into the yard, followed by all four of Zellaire's children. She liked the easy way he walked.

In the sudden rush of silence after the children left, Marie Therese dropped her hands into her lap.

She sighed tiredly and glanced at Gennie. "A handsome young man, is he not?"

"Mama, how can you say that? He's going off to fight against Frenchmen, didn't you hear?" Gennie felt angry and guilty at her own feelings.

"This afternoon you told me you hated Frenchmen."

"But I do not hate France," Gennie cried. "Papa and Phillippe are there somewhere!"

In this rare moment of solitude, mother and daughter exchanged glances that spoke volumes. At length Gennie said, "Mama, may I ask you something?"

"Anything, *ma petite.*"

"Do you think God is punishing us because we are not Catholics?"

"*Mon dieu!* Certainly not. Did not our Lord Jesus Christ also suffer for his beliefs? And didn't he talk directly with his people? His disciples did not keep him away from people."

Gennie pushed her wheel thoughtfully and began to spin again. "But the priests say—"

"Hah! They would have you believe that Jesus can be found only through their intervention. Doubt humans, *chérie,* but never doubt that Jesus loves us. All of us," Marie Therese said firmly. Then she smiled. "And hasn't he brought us to safe harbor? Could we have found a kinder gentleman than Monsieur Zellaire?"

When Gennie didn't answer, she said briskly, "Now, shall we get on with the supper for Monsieur Zellaire and his flock of goslings—and that nice Mr. Roebuck?"

She mixed a dough of flour and finely ground dried corn and dropped it by spoonsful on top of the stew simmering on Zellaire's new iron stove. She began to sing softly, one of Gennie's favorite hymns.

Gennie felt a surge of rebelliousness. How could her mother

sing? How could she pretend to be happy, even if M. Zellaire was a nice gentleman? She knew that he had lost his wife and the last baby in the epidemic. Yet the children's voices, outside, sounded happy. How could they be happy without their mother? How could her mother expect her ever to be happy without Papa and Phillippe?

Suddenly the door burst open. "Gennie, Gennie, I *need* you!"

It was Jean, the seven-year-old. He alone had found the way into her grieving heart. In her dreaming moments she imagined that Jesus had sent the love little Phillippe had had for her into Jean, for from the moment M. Zellaire had brought Marie Therese and Gennie home from Philadelphia, in his wagon, Jean had claimed her. He had simply walked up as she scrambled down from the high seat of the wagon and slipped his hand into hers, saying, "Will you help me find my top?"

That was something she had been able to do. Confronted by the strange red-haired man with his strange accent and by four noisy children—none of whose clothes seemed to fit, as if each upon arising merely grabbed what was nearest and put it on—Gennie had been relieved, almost eager, to respond to Jean's tugging and had allowed herself to led toward the tall grasses that grew around the well at the side of the house.

"Papa made my top for me," Jean had confided. "I was practicing making it spin, so I could do it for you." Jean had dropped to his knees. He looked up at her expectantly. With a small hesitation, Gennie obligingly followed. No sooner was she down than Jean's hand dove into the grass at the stone base of the well, and he yelled, "I found it!"

Gennie had to laugh. Jean scrambled to his feet and stood close to her, obviously waiting to be congratulated. She had hugged his plump middle as he looked seriously into her eyes. "Will you stay and not go away?"

"Until you are a big boy and don't need me any more," Gennie had responded. For she knew it was true. M. Zellaire had paid their passage and keep from France to England, and thence by long and dangerous sea journey to Penn's province (she still could not pronounce it). In return, her mother had signed papers indenturing them to M. Zellaire for seven years. *Seven years.*

"Gennie, *now!*" wheedled Jean, bringing her out of her reverie. The urgency in his voice bespoke not "I need you" but "I want to show you something."

Gennie smiled. She caught her mother watching.

"That child has you curled around his finger."

Gennie nodded. "He's so like Phillippe, isn't he, Mama?"

Her mother's eyes filled, and she looked away.

Gennie flipped her shawl from a peg by the door and allowed Jean to tug her outside.

Her gaze was drawn to the broad back of Mr. Thomas Roebuck. His legs were braced apart, his head cocked as he aimed the flintlock at a rock set up on a distant stump. There was a loud report. His shoulder took the recoil as the rock on the stump wobbled. The children cheered lustily.

"Papa's going to let me try it next," Jean confided. "You have to watch."

"All right." She watched Thomas load the rifle for Jean. Patiently he steadied the heavy barrel while the boy aimed and squeezed the trigger. The impact would have thrown him on the ground if Thomas had not been prepared to catch him. Then all the rest of the children begged turns. Zellaire tried to shoo them away, but Thomas shook his head good-naturedly. Zellaire threw his hands in the air and stood by while Thomas gave each a turn.

Unwillingly, Gennie had to admire his forbearance with the children. Her feelings were in turmoil. This brash man with his back turned had acted as if it were the most wonderful thing in the world to be going off to shoot Frenchmen. Catholics. Not Frenchmen. Catholics. Papists. Black Robes. She tried to conjure an image that she could hate and could not. A sigh escaped her. Why couldn't people just love Jesus and be done trying to make other people change?

Suddenly she turned and walked swiftly back into the warm house. "Mama, I have decided you are right. The young man is very brave to go off to war. Not so nice as Cousin 'Tienne, of course, but . . . And very wide shoulders, did you notice? And he was trying to be kind, wasn't he, by speaking French to me? Do you think he'll come back after the war, Mama?"

·C·H·A·P·T·E·R· 7·

homas Roebuck stayed for dinner with the Zellaires, trying not to wolf the savory stew and dumplings prepared by Madame Harmonie and served silently and with grace by Gennie. When Henri spoke the blessing, with the aroma of the piping stew rising in his nostrils, the quiet crack of logs in the fireplace, and its warmth on his back, Thomas experienced a rare moment of perfect tranquility. What a lucky man, Henri Zellaire, to have won such a family! The Frenchwomen fitted in like waters mingling in a handblown pitcher, adding sparkle and current.

"So you are going to Connecticut. You will follow the Appalachian Trail to the Hartford settlement?"

"Yes, sir. That is where the regiment is forming."

"I have a friend in Hartford. You must stay with him." Zellaire thought a moment and then chuckled, "In fact, he is the proprietor of the only decent tavern in Hartford, so you will indeed be staying with him. The Crown and Rose. I will send along a letter of introduction, if you like."

"Why, thank you, sir."

Zellaire's tongue explored the inner world of teeth and gums as he stared ruminatively at the smoke-darkened rafters. "As a matter of fact—yes. Thomas, lad, will you carry a personal letter also?"

"Of course, sir," Thomas mumbled through a full mouth, eyeing the second helping of stew Madame Harmonie was ladling on his plate.

"How long will you be away at the war, monsieur?"

Her voice from across the table surprised him. No longer restrained, it was musical and very clear. Gennie's eyes rested unwaveringly on his as she awaited his answer. Thomas smiled at her and pulled himself up straighter. "No longer than it takes to make the Papists give up, Miss Gennie."

"I suppose, once you show yourself, that will be no time at all," roared Zellaire.

Gennie flinched as if his loud voice frightened her.

"You will be coming back to Germantown then?" asked Madame Harmonie.

"Yes, ma'am. My folks have a section a few miles west of here."

He grinned cockily at Gennie. "We're 'bout as far as a body could be and still be counted civilized."

She looked away, not ready to be gay, but then irresistibly her eyes returned to his lively face. "Are you not afraid to live so close to the wilderness?"

"Sometimes it's better than living too close to folks. Some of 'em are not exactly trustworthy."

"Oh, so young to feel that way," protested Madame Harmonie. "One should not always say what one thinks."

"If that is what one thinks, why should one not say it?" Gennie said. "And he is right, you know he is!"

"I don't mean . . ." Thomas stammered, "Not like you folks . . ."

Zellaire came to his rescue. "Women will dissemble for hours rather than face the truth. You'll learn that." He climbed to his feet. "Now, I believe you offered a hand with the chores?"

"Yes, sir!"

As their boots crunched on the frozen path to the barn, Thomas bombarded Henri with questions about the Harmonies. His face grew somber as Zellaire related their story, concluding in a brisk voice, "It was a good investment for me, as you can see. Especially the mother. So good with the children. And such food! Have you ever tasted *pot au feu* like that? The herbs, did you notice? Marie Therese and Gennie planted an herb garden, from seeds brought from France." His eyes rolled heavenward. "The children love both of them, you can see that. They will be old enough to do for themselves before the seven years are up."

"What if someone came along and wanted to marry one or the other?"

Zellaire shrugged. "What could they do? Nothing. Without my permission, of course. If someone were willing to purchase the contract, say, of the daughter . . . Ah, here we are."

He tossed a pitchfork at Thomas and pointed down at the other end of the barn. Meanwhile he took another fork and began pitching hay into the milk cow's stall.

Thomas walked to the mule stalls. Seven years. He felt immensely sorry for the Frenchwomen. In seven years the mother would be old and worn. Who would take her in then? And Gennie would be past the marrying age and maybe would have to be a spinster or settle for someone much older, a widower most likely. Women alone did not have it easy; he could see that!

Something about Gennie attracted him. He smiled to think that such a little person had come to his defense at the supper table! No, not little exactly, because she was taller than her mother, but broken, perhaps, like a bird's wing that needed time to mend. He tossed a forkful of hay into the first mule's stall. She would want protecting. Hay into the second. She had no one! By the sweet, blessed Savior, she should have it! He drove the fork so violently into the ground that the handle vibrated back and forth, and seized a shovel to muck the stalls. Zellaire had no *right* to talk about them as if they were property!

He stopped and glanced to the other end of the barn, where Zellaire's red head bobbed up and down in the cow's stall. Why blame him? He had rescued them from life imprisonment in a convent! He was their benefactor. Didn't matter! Thomas was still angry. He worked furiously for several minutes, then gradually his pace slowed and he paused again.

How foolish to get his back up over someone he'd probably never see again. What was the matter with him? Didn't he own the finest, newest rifle invented? And wasn't he going off to just about the grandest adventure in the world? Now was not the time to go mooning about like a love-struck calf! He wondered if all Frenchwomen were like Gennie and Madame Harmonie.

Suddenly Thomas couldn't wait to shake off the dust of Germantown and be on his way.

·C·H·A·P·T·E·R·8·

he sign swinging in the slight breeze read: CROWN & ROSE, GEN. ISRAEL WALLINGHAM, PROP. Thomas depressed the latch and bent his head to enter. A rich rumble of masculine voices and a draught of warm air from the public room, to the left, swept into the cramped foyer, where he now stood.

"Good day, sir." A little maid with a starched, puckered cap set over a head of tight curls curtsied before him. "Shall ye be wanting dinner or lodging?"

Thomas pulled off his tricorn and began to unburden himself of knapsack and coat. "Both, please, miss. Is General Wallingham about?"

"Yes, sir."

"Give him this letter, please." As she left Thomas threw a yearning glance into the public room. A roaring fire lent a mellow glow to a portcullised bar, where three men stood at leisure, and illuminated two long trencher tables, both fully occupied.

His eyes were drawn to the colorful red-and-white uniforms of a quartet of English regimental officers at one table, who sat well apart from the provincials at the other end. The provincials, townspeople most likely, were garbed similarly to the citizens of Philadelphia, in dark broadcloth coats and breeches and woolen hose.

Several men huddled over a profusion of papers at the second table. The dishes had been shoved aside. Candles set in a candelabrum guttered over the papers. The men's faces were serious, their words smothered in the general geniality of the midday gathering.

Thomas shifted his grip on his flintlock and wondered whether it would be proper for him to keep it while he ate. He was reluctant to leave it now. In the days since leaving Germantown he had learned to trust it. Its accuracy amazed him. The balance that Zellaire had achieved seemed little short of miraculous. Pa's old musket could not compare.

He had reached Hartford near noon, after several days on foot. In Philadelphia he had traded the rest of his furs for a goodly number of shillings. Philadelphia was a great, grand place, with broad avenues and plenty of trees, now bare. There merchants bustled about from the docks, to the warehouses, to the streets, and Thomas had discovered row upon row of shops selling wonderful articles from England

41

and, if one found where to look, from France and the Indies as well.

Hartford was nearer the size of Germantown. There was a sprinkling of public buildings and more than one church. He even had to step out of the way for a carriage, pulled by two horses slushing down the middle of the partly frozen street. His leap had carried him in front of the window of one Elias Tidywell, PRINTER & SIGN-BOARD PAINTER, where he had read advertisements for stock, notices of rewards for runaway slaves and bondservants, meetings of the Ladies' Prayer Circle and the Hartford Gentlemen's Club.

Perhaps that was the Hartford Gentlemen's Club meeting right now in the public room. Thomas shifted his stance, feeling awkward and out of place. He had never been inside a public inn. Was he supposed to go inside with the others, as big as you please, as his mother might say?

"Mr. Roebuck." A sprightly gentlemen in the quiet dress of a town worthy came down the stairs and in two quick steps crossed the foyer. He looked up at Thomas with a warm smile, the grip of his hand as hearty as that of a much larger man. "I am General Wallingham. How is my young friend, Henri?"

Thomas smiled. "Very well, sir." Young friend! Henri Zellaire was old enough to be Thomas's father. But then General Wallingham appeared old enough to be his grandfather. The little man began issuing commands as if deploying forces on a battlefield. In short order he disposed of the questions of Thomas's possessions, his bed for the night, and had ordered a meal and a cup of warmed cider, after confirming that Thomas had only now walked up from Philadelphia.

Thomas was still carrying his rifle as he followed General Wallingham among the diners to a small, square table that the little maid carried and placed before the fire. General Wallingham had fought in the Cumberland Uprising twenty years earlier, he told him over his shoulder. Thomas presumed this was where he had acquired his rank.

After days of eating one meal a day, consisting of hard corn biscuits, jerked meat, and dried salt fish, Thomas's attention was entirely diverted from his garrulous host as the maid set before him heaping bowls of steaming boiled potatoes, squash, cabbage, a small joint of beef, a meat pie, and a tureen of chowder. He was literally slavering as he swept the first delicious spoonful of fish-and-potato chowder into his mouth.

Zellaire had apparently taken the liberty of telling the general of Thomas's plans, for pulling a second bench up to the table and discussing the present war at length while Thomas ate, Wallingham said suddenly, "One of the best leaders you will ever meet is right in this room."

His mouth full, Thomas swiveled toward the British officers.

Wallingham smiled. "The gentleman I speak of is Major General Roger Wolcott, commander of the Connecticut regiment." Wallingham flattened his fingers on the table and rubbed at an invisible circle. "Would you like to meet him?"

Thomas swallowed. "Me, sir? Yes, but why would he be interested in meeting me?"

Wallingham smiled again as if he had a private joke. "I like a man who is modest."

But he didn't answer the question, thought Thomas, regretfully leaving his unfinished dinner to follow the general to the table where earlier he had noted the serious men poring over papers.

"General Wolcott?"

Wolcott glanced up. Thomas saw a large head, a face with aquiline features and dark eyes, and dark, shoulder-length hair streaked with gray, tied in a queue. His clothing was not remarkable from his comrades'.

"I have an interesting young man here who has expressed a desire to meet you." Thomas threw Wallingham a startled look, which was not lost on Wolcott.

"Have you indeed?" Amusement kindled in his eyes, suggesting that he would welcome an interlude.

"Er—yes, sir."

"Why?"

Wallingham cut in smoothly. "Thomas Roebuck is a skilled woodsman and one of the very few who is an expert shot on *a new rifle.*"

Thomas stared at him in astonishment.

"In God's truth!" exclaimed Wolcott, now genuinely interested.

"Henri Zellaire, who is a gunsmith in Germantown, Pennsylvania, believes that were you to employ this rifle in your regiment, its efficacy would quickly become apparent."

Roebuck stood between the generals like a trapped lamb, his Adam's apple grown as huge as a melon, blocking any protest. What would the general think when he found out the truth? His eyes flashed angrily at Wallingham, who seemed to care not a whit.

"Where are you from, Roebuck?"

"My father's farm, west of Germantown, sir."

"And your famous rifle, you have it with you now?"

"Yes, sir." It was propped against his own little table, by his cooling dinner. With a sigh, Thomas fetched it. "The gunsmith calls it a flintlock, sir."

Wolcott eyed it with interest but made no move. "Hm. You came all the way to Hartford to join the Connecticut regiment?"

"Yes, sir. I stopped here first to pay respects to Mr. Zellaire's friend General Wallingham."

Standing with proprietary pride next to Thomas, Wallingham placed both hands behind his back and studied the ceiling.

A faint smile trembled on Wolcott's lips as his glance flickered to his fellow officers. Suddenly he rose and clapped a hand on Thomas's shoulder. He was slightly taller than Thomas and of a vigorous build.

"Have you finished your meal?"

"No, sir." Roebuck was beginning to feel confused by the order of questions.

"No matter! Will you now honor us with a demonstration of your new piece?"

Even as Wolcott asked, he propelled Roebuck, who cast a regretful glance at his first good meal in over a week, from the public room. Coats and capes magically appeared, and before he knew it, Thomas had been hustled outside and behind the inn.

Wolcott and his officers were interested in every phase of loading the flintlock. Absorbed in sharing his pleasure and pride in his new rifle, Thomas forgot his outrage at the exaggerations of the old general and even began to swell a bit as each man—and all were older than he by a half-dozen years—listened intently to his explanations and then tried his gun for himself. None was as accurate as he, who had had two weeks' practice. For a *pièce de résistance*, Thomas aimed at a squirrel that had unfortunately chosen that moment to pause at the edge of the trees, a little more than two hundred yards away. In a miraculous shot, Thomas dropped it. He tried to act nonchalant about the unheard-of luck of his shot.

"By Jove, lad!"

"Good shooting! What a piece, Roger!"

The men's voices grew younger with excitement.

"How old are you, Roebuck?"

Thomas almost blurted the truth before thinking quickly, feeling that age bestowed dignity, and answering, "Nearly twenty, sir." Not quite a lie. Of course he would be nearly twenty for another two years.

"I see."

Now what was Wolcott leading up to? Did he think him too young to fight?

"And you think you will be a better soldier than farmer?"

"My father says a man should know how to protect his land."

"And what do you think?"

Thomas frowned. "Why, 'tis the truth, sir. If we be not willing to forego our daily chores and fight the French now, we'll only have to do it later."

"Oh? Whence did you receive this wisdom, young Roebuck?"

"My father, sir. When we have taught the French a lesson, I will go back to Pennsylvania. But west, beyond the Allegheny Mountains. I want to see the river called Ohio."

"*La Belle Rivière*," Wolcott murmured. He assessed Thomas silently. "I am thinking that it was a knowing Providence that sent you to me. I like the way you handle that flintlock. We have only five hundred men in all the Connecticut regiment. I will make you my junior gunnery officer, with rank of lieutenant. Your pay will be twelve shillings a month; you provide clothing and equipment. Lodging and food will be supplied by the regiment. Well?"

"An officer, sir? *Me*? But I—*yes, sir!*"

"Good. Come, let's inside before we freeze our buttocks. As soon as possible, I want you to return to your Mr. Zellaire and arrange for the regiment to purchase all the flintlocks and balls he has. If there are other gunsmiths about who are making the rifle, engage their stores also. That will be your job."

He threw a grim smile at the others. "Our job will be to convince the Connecticut legislature to pay for them. We will work out the details before you leave. Sparhawk!"

A tall, wiry young man, who sported an immense, elegant moustache, was immediately at his side. "Yes, sir?"

"Get Roebuck settled. Take him along tomorrow when you drill the men."

Thomas was in a spin. In Hartford less than half a day, and he was already an officer in the Connecticut regiment! He could hardly wait to write his family. Suddenly he thought of Gennie. He pictured himself riding through the gate in the stone wall. He began to imagine what he would say to her.

"Roebuck!"

"Yes, General Wolcott?"

Wolcott grinned. "I'd give a dram of rum to know the meaning of that silly smile that just left your face."

"No, ye wouldn't, sir. She be too young for ye!"

he first fine Saturday in early spring 1745, Henri Zellaire loaded the four children and Marie Therese and Gennie into the wagon and drove to town. The rutted, damp streets were bustling with neighbors and civilized Indians, as well as the newest immigrants from northern Europe. To one and all he called "Good morning!" was if well pleased to be showing off his handsome new servants.

Embarrassed by the attention he was drawing, Gennie nevertheless resisted the impulse to duck her head on the ticking, which covered a thick layer of straw where she sat with the children in the bed of the wagon. There was so much that was new to see! Men of berry-tint skin wandered through town, with few clothes on, though the air was chilly. A cluster of men with their backs to the street seemed to be reading a newspaper tacked up outside the Germantown Hotel. Her heart flipped into her stomach momentarily as she thought she recognized a stocky figure with curly black hair tied in a queue. She half rose in the wagon. No. It wasn't he. Her ears were assaulted by the teasing voices of two youths, yelling at each other in their broad and indelicate English tongue, as near to French as a leathered fist to a satin glove.

Zellaire pulled the wagon up before the largest building on the street, built of vertical gray board, with the single word *mercantile* painted in heavy black letters on a yellow sign, which was mounted over the door and two windows. He bustled them all across six feet of porch and inside.

"Mr. Amos! Goodman Amos, meet my servant, Madame Flourinot Harmonie." Zellaire's watery blue eyes glowed with pride. "And show us some bolts of cloth. Madame Harmonie was a seamstress in France."

Gennie and Marie Therese exchanged glances. Gennie felt color flooding her cheeks. Her poor mother! She remembered the night that M. Zellaire had first realized that her mother was an accomplished seamstress as well as a thrifty goodwife. He had examined a seam or two, thrown the garment in the air, seized up Jean, and whirled him around the room. Marie Therese had not known what to think. As she told Gennie later, they were but farm women, come down to indenture, and every goodwife could sew! Who was M. Zellaire thinking to impress with such a fuss?

Gennie squeezed her mother's fingers in sympathy as their master carried on in the mercantile. She knew how her mother pined for friends among the womenfolk of Germantown. M. Zellaire certainly was not helping! Suddenly Gennie's eye was caught by a bolt of luscious pink wool—English, it must be—balanced on a stack of several other bolts of sober hue that Goodman Amos was bringing to the counter.

"Mother, look! Isn't it beautiful?" Eagerly she fingered the goods. They both looked at Zellaire.

Leaning against the counter, his legs negligently crossed, Zellaire gave the appearance of fancying himself a young rake. "Well, Madame Harmonie, find something to your liking? The gray ought to do, don't you think?"

Delicately Marie Therese pressed Henri's sleeve with the backs of her fingers. "*Oui, monsieur,* but I was also thinking. . . . Have your little girls had anything pretty since their mother passed? I could make each of them, and my daughter, too, *comme il faut,* a dress that would be just as serviceable, and they would be so pretty!" Madame Harmonie smiled at him with exactly the right amount of hope and trust.

Gennie stared openmouthed at her mother. Why, she was looking at M. Zellaire just as she had used to look at Papa sometimes.

Zellaire was acutely aware of the envious eyes of other men and of their wives. What he said now would be repeated in both the alehouses of Germantown tonight! The silence grew thick.

Gennie glanced at the gray-haired gentleman behind the counter. She caught his eyes upon her, filled with naked hunger. Hastily she averted her eyes, conscious that his bold stare was continuing. How rude he was! Her cheeks flamed, and she concentrated her gaze on the shelves stuffed haphazardly with goods.

Amos watched the color flood her cheeks and was pleased at her reaction. He bounced gently on the balls of his feet. *She is wondering,* he thought, *why a man of my standing would bother noticing the likes of her.*

"We'll have the rose, Amos. The whole bolt, please!"

Amos tore his thoughts from Gennie. "All of it, Henri?"

"The whole bolt, Monsieur Zellaire?" protested Marie Therese. "But surely . . ."

"*You* shall have a dress, too!"

"But you must allow for linen for the boys' shirts."

"A bolt of fine linen, too, Amos!" He turned to her again and said in a none-too-low voice, "A shirt for the master of the house, too, eh?"

Shocked whispers and titters greeted this bold statement.

Marie Therese rewarded him with a dazzling smile, not lost on the other shoppers. "One, at least, monsieur!"

Gennie glanced past her mother's shoulder. The man would not cease his staring! Finally she asked, "Shall I take the children outside?" Zellaire nodded, and she hurried the brood into the flood of spring sunshine. She breathed a grateful sigh. The air was fragrant and crisp. One could ignore the puddles of mud, could forgive the snow for melting so messily, for the savor of such a day!

A dark-skinned, young-looking woman was watching her with friendly curiosity. When Gennie returned her smile, she sauntered over.

"Good day. I am Rosalind Hambleton." Her voice was richly accented. Her lips curved with the well-defined beauty of the West Indian. The plain linsey-woolsey skirt and jacket of the house servant seemed out of place on her.

"What a beautiful name." Gennie switched unconsciously to French.

Rosalind Hambleton did likewise. "Thank you. I chose it myself, and Mr. Hambleton said I could keep it."

"You chose your own name?"

"Sometimes a body has to do things for herself." She glanced over her shoulder, through the dim doorway of the mercantile. "That Mr. Amos is sure taken with you."

Gennie shuddered. "I do not like the way he looks at me."

Rosalind shrugged. "He is rich."

"He is old enough to be my grandfather. Almost." They both laughed at the image.

"Old enough to buy your contract," Rosalind persisted.

"How do you know so much about me? I don't know the first thing about you!"

"Told you 'most all there is. I work for the Hambletons. Got my own little place on their property. He bought me proper."

A frown hovered over Gennie's brow. "He did? For seven years?"

"Forever, girl. You ought to set your cap for that old man."

"No!"

"If you can get him to marry you, he will protect you. And when he dies, you will be free. Maybe with a little property of your own. Won't be no seven years, either," she added, with a judicious glance back at the shop.

Involuntarily Gennie pictured herself in Mr. Amos' bed. She

shuddered. "I would rather work out my seven years." Life with Mr. Zellaire's family suddenly did not seem so terrible. "I love the children as if they were my own kin."

"He could sell your contract any time he took it in his head, girl."

"He wouldn't!"

"No?" A cynical smile lifted one corner of Rosalind's exquisite lips. "Then wait till he climbs in your bed one cold night."

Gennie gasped.

"Then who'll you run to?"

"Well, here we are!" Marie Therese bustled out of Goodman Amos' Mercantile, her arms filled with string-wrapped packages. Her spirits were higher than Gennie had seen them for months. "Henri is settling his account. We are to fetch the family into the wagon and wait for him."

Gennie threw a troubled glance at Rosalind Hambleton just as Zellaire and another gentleman emerged from the store.

"Ye won't have her long, Zellaire," the other one was saying with a laugh. "Even the skinny ones get married right out from under your nose."

Rosalind's perfect eyebrows arched upward. "Come see me if you need someone to talk to sometime," she murmured. "Just ask for the midwife's place."

Marie Therese missed the exchange, and Gennie hurried to help her get the children in the wagon. Gennie climbed in back with the children as Zellaire gallantly helped Marie Therese up to the springboard.

The wagon swayed back and forth on the mushy road. Its rhythm tilted Marie Therese's upright body against Zellaire's sturdy shoulder, back and forth. She threw an encouraging smile, over her shoulder, at her daughter, meant to reassure her of her love. Gennie did not return the smile. They were due for a good, old-fashioned heart-to-heart, Marie Therese decided.

Perhaps in throwing herself into their new life and trying to make it a happier one for all, she had neglected Gennie. Marie Therese took a deep, appreciative draught of the pure, scented air. Perhaps it was no more than Gennie needing a dose of physic. Who could be unhappy long in this beautiful country?

The crudeness of Rosalind's words had paralyzed Gennie. Perhaps she had not meant to be cruel, only to warn her. What could she do? Dear sweet Jesus! And the shameful way her mother was behaving, almost touching Mr. Zellaire as they swayed with the wagon! She probably wouldn't care if he did decide to sell her contract.

Miserably Gennie drew her knees up under her petticoats and hugged them, not caring that the two boys had begun to quarrel and might awaken the girls, who had fallen asleep on the ticking. *I will pray for Papa to come*, she decided. If one prayed with steadfastness, never doubting, then nothing else could possibly happen.

·C·H·A·P·T·E·R· 10 ·

ood luck and Godspeed, Thomas!" Peter Sparhawk stepped back from the carriage with a half salute.

"I'll see you in Boston!"

With a cry and a crack of the whip, Sandy McGinnis's heavy carriage gathered speed and thundered down the post road from Hartford toward Philadelphia.

Thomas settled back, nodded at the other five men who were his fellow passengers, and wondered how he was going to keep the dust off his new coat.

In the weeks Thomas had been at Hartford, Lieutenant Peter Sparhawk had taken him under his wing. Darkly handsome and something of a dandy, Peter's last act of kindness had been to haul Thomas to a tailor and have an impressive coat made. Sparhawk, scion of a Massachusetts whaling family, thought nothing of ordering several coats, with matching breeches, gloves, and hats, for himself at the same time.

What would William Roebuck have said at his son spending nearly all his hoarded fur money to put green wool broadcloth on his back, with two rows of brass buttons yet?

"Never mind about him!" Sparhawk had said airily. "The men must have you looking like an officer, Roebuck."

As it was, British regulars paid scant respect to colonial officers. The mere rank and file were ignored entirely. Having little idea what they were doing going to war, the provincial farmers and coopers and haberdashers lining up to drill on village greens across the colonies tried vainly to imitate their British counterparts.

The British regulars were masters at close-order drill. Twenty abreast, they could kneel and reload while twenty more standing behind them fired a volley as one. The fine, polished black boots, snug white trousers, and imperial red coat with gold braid and buttons set the British soldier apart as much as the oiled and blued Brown Bess shouldered so smartly.

Most of the colonists wore homespun shirts and trousers of drab gray, with heavy woolen overshirts extending past the hips, overlapped a handspan or more at the waist to form, when belted, a pouch for personal items. Over this each slung his powder horn and his pouch with balls and tinder.

The superior attitudes of the British regulars toward the volunteers left the Americans with a distaste of anything to do with British military precision. At times it was as if the Continentals went out of their way to be considered rude, uncouth, and totally lacking in civilized graces.

"Don't let that fool you, Roebuck," Sparhawk had cautioned him. "Our men may not know how to make war, but they know the land and the people, and they are not too proud to learn! A leader who does not respect these qualities deserves to lose his men."

On his first day with the troops, gazing out over the Hartford green where Wolcott's 500 volunteers had fallen out, Thomas felt sudden panic. There were frontiersmen in buckskin, more at home on lonely Indian paths than in company; there were austere schoolteacher-parsons and timid store clerks; rugged mule drivers and a few civilized Indians, reverting from broadcloth to warpaint for the occasion.

Lieutenant Sparhawk nudged his horse forward. "Attention!" he shouted from the back of a Narragansett pacer temporarily donated to the regiment by a patriotic horsebreeder.

Only the first ranks heard him. He shouted again and waved his arms, motions that were repeated by those in front for the benefit of those behind. Finally a rough sort of order was achieved.

They behave as if they are on holiday, Thomas thought.

"For those of you who just joined, I am Lieutenant Peter Sparhawk, adjutant to Major General Roger Wolcott."

In a few minutes, Sparhawk had efficiently dispensed assignments and orders of the day and told off thirty or forty men and ordered them aside. The rest broke into their companies.

Sparhawk turned to the remaining group. These were men who already carried arms. Only half carried them with ease of familiarity. By their dress, they were the frontiersmen.

"You men are going to be issued the finest rifles in the world, just as fast as we can procure them. Lieutenant Roebuck here is an expert with the new rifle. He will teach you how to shoot it, and just as important, since some of you have never handled a piece like it before, how to care for it." Sparhawk turned to Roebuck. "All yours, lieutenant."

Thomas's heart was pounding. The sea of faces looking up at him all seemed older, in years and experience. He would not dare make a mistake. What if the men would not follow him?

"You'll find, lad, that until you get the men to like you, you'll have little success with them," Wolcott had advised him earlier. "Learn their names and more. Don't be afraid to call up the ones with superior ability. Remember, the lads are volunteers. They can up and leave. And when you finish each day, order an issue of rum around. Be swift in discipline, be hearty in praise, be fair. And ask for the blessing of Providence each morning to lighten your task."

O sweet Providence, Thomas prayed, *show me how to win the men to my command!* He held up a hand for attention. "The first thing . . ." His voice squeaked and broke, a mortifying thing that had not happened for five years. He thought illogically how glad he was that his father was not there to witness it. He coughed and began again, thinking suddenly of Gennie.

"Think of your rifle as your lady, to be treated with respect and gentleness, to be sheltered from harsh elements—"

A grizzled frontiersman, with long, sun-bleached hair and porcupine-quill decorated buckskins, grinned at him displaying a mouth with teeth broken or missing. "Make love to it? That right, lieutenant?"

Guffaws broke out around him, and Thomas laughed. "Only if you can teach it to kiss."

The men elbowed each other, pleased at his wit. They began to relax. Thomas grinned. He swung off his horse and handed the reins to one of the men. "Gather round. . . ," and he began to take the rifle apart, piece by piece, and patiently explain its workings.

Major General Roger Wolcott had moved his command headquarters from the public tavern to a tent in the midst of the camp. Military tents were largely nonexistent, but his staff had procured quantities of used sailcloth, and a town of odd-sized tents sprang up next to the Hartford green.

Thomas's job began with rifle drill and ended with hunting detail. He did not envy other lieutenants and sergeants whose tasks were to persuade hardy and independent men of the necessity of digging latrines and garbage pits, rounding up from the community quantities of food in exchange for military chits, or arranging cooking and policing details. He enjoyed working with his men and as the weeks passed grew more confident of their abilities as well as his own.

As the coach rocked along, Thomas was thinking of the growing success of their hunting details. That alone had enhanced the reputation of the flintlock. He wondered how many more he would be able to procure from Zellaire, now that General Wolcott had succeeded in prying the money out of the legislature.

In early afternoon the coach pulled into a tavern yard for dinner. Thomas was ravenous, although the name of the tavern, the Croaking Crow, did not exactly enhance one's appetite.

"Half hour, no more," sang McGinnis as he sprang down, calling two boys from the stables. "Step lively, lads, tend the horses!"

Immediately they sprang forward with buckets of water, as though well familiar with McGinnis's routine. The driver strode into the tavern ahead of his passengers, who paused in the yard to wash up.

When Thomas and the others trooped in, Thomas caught a glimpse of McGinnis sitting in the kitchen with a plump goodwife, eating heartily. A parson hurried forward.

"Welcome, travelers. How fortunate that I happen to be passing my dinner hour among God-fearing, sober, and pious gentlemen such as yourselves. Gentlemen, if you will be seated, I will ask God's blessing upon our fare."

Eagerly the travelers found places at the trencher table in the public room. The parson cleared his throat. He began to speak. On and on he spoke.

Thomas fidgeted. He cast surreptitious glances toward the rear of the tavern, whence emanated tantalizing aromas. He chided himself. And why should he be thinking of his stomach, when his spiritual life was no doubt in greater need? At last the parson sat down, and a lad entered through a door, carrying a tray of pewter mugs and pitchers of steaming cider. He was followed immediately by another lad wearing a huge apron bearing a platter of meat and biscuits.

A plate heaped with stewed meat, vegetables, and gravy appeared before Thomas. He seized his spoon, the only utensil afforded by the host, and a slab of Indian bread and set to.

At that moment McGinnis's head appeared through the kitchen doorway. "All aboard, lads!" Howls of protest greeted this order. "I told ye, half an hour, no more! My coach runs on schedule. Folks can set their timepieces by McGinnis, and they knows it. Look lively now, or remain behind!"

If there was any doubt he meant what he said, it was dispelled by the sounds of the stable boys backing the horses into their harnesses.

The parson took no notice of the men's protests, but went on complacently eating. Thomas noticed as he resentfully stuffed his pouch with Indian bread and headed for the coach how contentedly, too, the driver was wiping his mouth. Something in their performances was too pat.

For the rest of the trip, Thomas noticed with wry delight, none of the passengers took time to wash up before meals. They washed after, if there was time.

In Philadelphia Thomas left the coach and engaged a horse for the short journey out to Germantown.

iding out of Philadelphia for Germantown, Thomas's thoughts turned increasingly to the Huguenot girl living at Zellaire's. He realized she had been with him even when he was occupied with other things. Of course he had seen her only briefly that first visit. Maybe her appeal was just in his mind. Maybe it was the lack of young ladies on the parade ground that kept her image before him.

Suddenly Thomas spied another rider on the post road directly ahead. He spurred gently to catch up. The other seemed quite old, though stout and hardy. Thomas introduced himself.

"Thomas Roebuck, is it? Is your father the farmer with a section west of Germantown?"

"Yes, sir."

The stout man nodded. He was well dressed. His coat was of a fine black broadcloth. His white stock and cuffs were edged with white embroidery. His gray trousers matched his tricorn, and his silk hose were as black as the soft, ankle-top boots. A person of importance, Thomas decided.

"I had the privilege once of coming to your father's aid. Betimes, perhaps, I will again." He peered at Thomas. "The mercantile?"

"You would not be Mr. Goodman Amos?"

Amos glanced up at the sharp inflection in his voice. "I am."

Thomas swallowed. When would he learn not to betray his feelings! His father *had* talked of a certain proprietor of a mercantile in Germantown.

Three years past, William Roebuck had broken his ankle in a fall from the roof. All Thomas recalled (from straining to hear whispered talk between his parents at night) was that Pa had somehow gotten into debt to Amos, who had charged him usurious rates to advance goods before payment. Yes. And Amos had made certain the townspeople knew who it was that had given Roebuck credit rather than see the poor fellow set in the stocks for nonpayment. "I'd have been a sight better off in the stocks," Roebuck had groused in the children's hearing as he toted up the extra charges, "since I am laid up at any cost."

"Had you business in Philadelphia?" Amos was inquiring.

So this was Goodman Amos. With an effort, Thomas answered

him with the respect due an elder. "No, sir. I am an officer in the Connecticut regiment, traveling on military business for General Wolcott."

If Amos was impressed, he had no difficulty concealing it. "A bunch of tomfool nonsense, that. Over yet?"

"Oh, no, sir."

"Humph. Well, I shall be glad for the company of a neighbor's youngster. I am bound for Henri Zellaire's place. Know it?"

Youngster? He disliked Amos more each time he opened his mouth. "Yes, I know it."

If Thomas had wondered at Amos' surprising warmth upon realizing a traveling companion, he hadn't long to discover the reason. Apparently electing himself Thomas's mentor, Amos proceeded to instruct him, mile after tedious mile, in the proper conduct of business matters, as well as filial duties. Thomas had not attended the conversation for several minutes when Amos's words brought him up sharply.

"Frenchwomen? You mean the two gentlewomen whom Mr. Zellaire has taken in?"

His companion threw him a complacent smile. "Naturally. The welfare of persons of delicate breeding who have fallen on unfortunate times concerns us all."

Thomas was bewildered. These charitable words scarcely fit the Goodman Amos his father raged against! Well. If Amos had business with Zellaire, that would give Thomas leave to hang about and visit with Gennie until the old man finished. He smiled. Providence favors the young!

As last the tired horses turned in at the stone stile marking Zellaire's property. Two little boys playing marbles beside the stile watched them ride in.

Jean Zellaire scrambled to his feet. "Good afternoon, Mr. Amos." He grinned shyly at Thomas, evidently not recalling his name. Suddenly he sped for the house, shouting, "Madame! Madame! Company!"

The other child squinted up against the sun and inquired gravely if he might put up the horses.

Suddenly Thomas sighted Gennie in the doorway. She was clad in a woolen dress of deep rose. Her dark hair was pulled under a starched, ruffled white cap, from which wisps of brown curl had escaped and lay charmingly on her slender neck, and about her ears. The rose color coaxed matching color into her cheeks and lips. A sigh escaped his lips. He had never seen anyone so pretty.

At the sight of him, Gennie's lips parted in a glad, ingenuous smile. As an afterthought she curtsied. "Mr. Roebuck!"

Thomas dismounted, swept off his hat, and grinned. "Miss Harmonie. Good day, Madame Harmonie," he added as Marie Therese appeared behind her daughter.

"What a pleasant surprise. We did not expect to see you again so soon."

"You look so—so big!" added Gennie.

"It's this coat. Like it? Most of the officers wear them. You don't think this green is too bright, do you?"

Goodman Amos cut between them. "That dress is very nice, Miss Harmonie, very nice indeed." He examined her with a frank and critical eye. "My goods were just what was needed."

Two little girls crowded around Gennie's skirts. They also wore dresses of the rose-colored cloth.

What was going on here? To give away expensive goods on behalf of refugees was very generous indeed! His father *must* have misjudged Goodman Amos!

Madame Harmonie said, "Children, do not block the doorway. Let our guests in!"

Roebuck imagined her smile faltered slightly when she greeted Amos. For himself there was no doubt her pleasure was real. Zellaire, it turned out, was expected momentarily, having gone to help a neighbor whose cow was calving with difficulty.

"Sit by the fire, Mr. Amos. Mr. Zellaire would want me to offer you some refreshment."

Gratefully Amos lowered his bulk to a sturdy rush chair by the hearth. Marie Therese turned to Gennie. "Gennie, dear, please fetch some cheese from the dairy cellar."

Goodman Amos scuffled to his feet on the instant. "Allow me to carry it for you, Miss Harmonie."

"Nonsense!" Gaily Madame Harmonie pushed him back into his chair. "Mr. Roebuck would be happy to help, would you not, Mr. Roebuck?"

"It is my sincere pleasure," he said, only too conscious that he was employing the best manners he could muster.

Gennie had not looked at any of them during this exchange. She slipped her shawl off a peg and threw it around her shoulders. She went through the door and shut it firmly after Thomas before any of the children took it in their heads to follow. Finally she glanced at him. Her lips parted with a soft blowing sound. Her eyes flickered with momentary gaiety.

When she brushed close to him, Thomas caught the scent of a sweet fragrance that reminded him of spring flowers.

"Mama has saved me again! Mr. Amos believes it is his duty to teach me everything in history, as well as to correct my speech and penmanship."

Thomas laughed. "It was the same with me, all the way from Philadelphia. Your English has become very good, much better than my French. How long is it now since you left France?"

Gennie hesitated, and Thomas realized he had blundered. She probably did not want to talk about that. But then she said, "Seven months. Last autumn. It was the beginning of the harvest season . . ."

Suddenly they were talking as easily as if they had grown up together. Remembering last time, Thomas had worried that he would not know what to say to her when they did meet.

Slowly Gennie led the way through the kitchen garden to the dairy cellar, which was under the house but accessible only through an outside door.

"You look so pretty, Miss Harmonie . . . Gennie."

"Thank you. Mr. Zellaire took the whole bolt of wool, so Mama made dresses for all of us. The children think it is a game, to all wear our rose dresses at the same time." She threw Thomas a happy smile. "Little boys do not play such games as dress up, do they? My brother never did."

"Well, we did, after a fashion, but I suppose one would call it 'dress down.' Depending on who got to be the Indian." He felt her nearness as a giddy, pleasurable sensation. They reached the dairy cellar. He swung back the heavy trap door and felt a blast of chill air. Gennie quicky descended the mossy, stone steps and reappeared moments later, carrying a golden cheese, ripe and bulging in a string net. Thomas closed the door and held out his hands for the cheese.

Their fingers grazed as she gave it to him, and he felt it like a shock of cold water. They stood gazing at each other.

Gennie studied him. His face was square, blunt featured, with a good strong jaw and honest eyes. She liked the way his mouth was ready to lift into a smile at any excuse. It made her feel happy, she realized in surprise. "I tried to remember what you looked like after you left last time."

"You did?" He laughed self-consciously, pleased.

"Your eyes are cornflower blue, not gray blue. No one in my family has blue eyes."

He grinned. "It's from the Irish, I guess. Along with the black hair."

Gennie lifted a forefinger, as if to touch his face. Instead she placed it delicately against her small front teeth. She smiled.

Thomas leaned in to her, fighting an urge to sweep her into his arms. He had the intuitive feeling it would frighten her. He noticed the sprinkling of freckles across her small nose and her cold-reddened cheeks. A crisp wind teased the curls around her ears. He swallowed.

"Oh, Gennie." Impulsively he touched the soft line of her jaw, below the ear. She dipped her head and rubbed it against his hand, like a cat. "I thought of you all the time," he said huskily.

She tore her gaze away and looked out across the cold-deadened valley. Her mood seemed to change. She reached across her breasts and pulled the shawl closer. "You probably should not think of me."

"Why not?"

"You know."

"I do not."

"Because I am not free, Mr. Roebuck." Her voice was soft and low, but with an underlying edge of firmness. "I have no right to my own friends. I am—for seven years—I am no better than a slave. . . . And then I shall be old and ugly!" she burst out. She turned away, her body straight.

Thomas turned her by the shoulders to face him. Tears were tunneling down her rigid cheeks. He fumbled for a handkerchief. "Gennie, don't . . ." Balancing the heavy cheese in one arm he blotted awkwardly at her face. "I'll talk to your mother."

"She cannot help. She is as powerless as I."

"Or Mr. Zellaire, then. Or Mr. Amos. He was kind enough to give you the bolt of cloth, perhaps he—"

"Oh, Mr. Roebuck!" Gennie's voice rang with despair. "Mr. Zellaire bought those goods, but to hear Mr. Amos tell it . . . oh, I am so wicked! Why can I not just thank my blessed Jesus that I am here safe, as Mama says, and—and trust in his love!"

"But I don't—"

"Please, Mr. Roebuck, let us get back to the house!" Gennie whirled out of his grasp and ran back to the house.

After a moment, Thomas followed, bewildered by her behavior, trying to recall what it was he had said.

Zellaire had returned while they were fetching the cheese and now insisted that Amos and Roebuck stay for supper. Thomas decided to bide his time. He would find out what was so sorely troubling Gennie—if not tonight, then before he joined the regiment in Boston.

"Well, Thomas," Henri Zellaire said. His red hair and fair, freckled cheeks gleamed in the firelight. The children had left the table, the adults lingering on the benches after supper. Zellaire felt in great good humor. His flintlock had been a great success, as he had known it would. "Now tell us what is really going on up the coast. You are off to Boston, are you?"

Thomas glanced at Marie Therese. "Yes, Mr. Zellaire, but perhaps Madame Harmonie and Gennie would rather not hear war talk."

"We understand," said Marie Therese. "You are speaking of French Catholics in Canada and not our France."

"My cousin Etienne is somewhere in New France," ventured Gennie.

"Is he a priest?"

Gennie smiled. "No. He is a coureur de bois."

Thomas was about to ask if Etienne knew she was here when Goodman Amos said, "Ah, yes. The Papists are interested in two things here in the New World. Souls and skins. Not necessarily in that order." He looked around expectantly, as if pleased with his own wittiness.

Zellaire leaned forward from the head of the table. "We French can always be proud of the priests who came to New France. Never were men braver than those early Black Robes. I recall—"

"Explorers with the best of them," agreed Amos. "One time the Iroquois surprised some coureurs and their Huron friends. Father Jogue was with them, but out of camp, when his friends were captured. Do you know what he did, Gennie?" Amos fastened his eyes on hers and ran his tongue over his lower lip.

Catching her mother's cautionary glance, Gennie shook her head.

"He said to himself, 'My Huron friends have accepted our Lord. And the Iroquois are pagan butchers. So I will be serving both tribes if I go with them.' And he followed them and gave himself up! To the Iroquois! Hah! You can bless the fact the Iroquois love the English more than they hate the French Catholics."

Amos took the liberty of patting Gennie's clenched hand, where it rested on the edge of the tablecloth. "The Iroquois were happy enough to have another prisoner. They treated him terribly, but they couldn't break his spirit. 'Twas the Dutch finally rescued him. Well then the dim fool goes back to France and shows the king how they pulled all his fingernails out and—"

Gennie shuddered. "Please, Mr. Amos!" Everyone knew that Father Jogue had come back to New France, determined to bring the savages to know their blessed Lord, and that the next time the Iroquois caught him they killed him. She never wanted to hear any more about people dying.

Seeing the stricken look on her face, Thomas stood up. "Gennie, would you care to walk?" He couldn't understand Amos. The man looked as if he relished the anguish he was causing. Didn't he know what the Harmonies had themselves suffered? Where was his Christian charity?

"Why don't you see the little ones to bed, Gennie?" Henri suggested. "And turn in yourself. You look a bit pale."

"Yes, monsieur."

Zellaire turned to Thomas and rubbed his hands together. "Well, Thomas. This is not merely a social call for you, is it? Shall we leave the others to digest their suppers and get on to business?"

"Of course, sir." Thomas tried in vain to catch Gennie's eye as she herded the children upstairs. Amos was watching her, too, still standing at the table, with his teeth bared in a strange smile. Thomas glanced quickly at Marie Therese. She apparently did not notice the old man's behavior.

"Ah-hum," sighed Amos, removing himself to his chair by the fire as Marie Therese began to pick up the pewter and wood dishes.

Time was running against him. His family expected him yet tonight; he had to finish arrangements with Zellaire; and he knew with dismal certainty that Gennie would not show herself again downstairs until Amos left. She seemed almost afraid of him. With these thoughts drumming about in his head, Thomas reluctantly followed Zellaire into the workshop.

Zellaire had fourteen flintlocks in various stages of completion. After they had agreed upon price, Thomas confessed he would have to seek out other gunsmiths. General Wolcott hoped to supply at least 100 of his men with the superior rifle.

Through the doorway between workshop and living room, Thomas could see Amos and Marie Therese, him droning on, with an occasional comment from her as she bent over her sewing. Zellaire had not responded to his last remark, so Thomas said forthrightly, "You must know of other gunsmiths in this valley who make flintlocks. I can find them, but it will take less time if you tell me."

Zellaire's tongue explored his cheek, and he studied the rafters, which were stacked with varying lengths of drying hardwoods. Finally he gave Thomas a rueful glance.

"Lad, I would say you nay if I could supply all you need. Since I cannot . . . before I tell you, you must promise me the price we agreed upon remains confidential. I'll not have you bandying about my price to gain leverage with others."

Thomas busied himself examining a gleaming gray barrel to con-

ceal his confusion. Why would Zellaire make such a request? Unless
. . . of course. He must be fearful that the others would learn what a
low price Zellaire had given him out of friendship, and gain a laugh at
Zellaire's expense. Relieved, Thomas smiled expansively.

"You can trust me," he said.

·C·H·A·P·T·E·R· 12 ·

rom the dormer, Gennie watched Thomas leave. Her heart made strange flip-flops as horse and rider disappeared at a leisurely pace into the shadows of the trees. He was so handsome! So kind! He had come to her defense when that awful Mr. Amos . . . But he had several miles to go to reach his father's place, hadn't he said? Was it quite safe? Mr. Zellaire should have insisted he stay!

Goodman Amos' high-pitched laugh intruded in her pleasure. She glanced at Nabby and Daisy, fast asleep in their bed, and crept to the door of the girls' bedroom. She opened it a crack.

". . . just a girl," she heard Zellaire say.

"My first wife had our first child before she was that age," said Amos' voice.

Her hand froze on the latch. And then her mother, the words a low murmur, the tone temporizing. The words of Rosalind Hambleton came back to her, and Gennie's heart raced. It was happening just as she said! Amos *could* buy her. Of course! Zellaire did not really need her, not with her mother. He had accepted her because Sister Margarethe had pledged mother and daughter would not be separated.

Oh, sweet Lord Jesus, what could she do? She would die before she would consent to marry a man like Goodman Amos. She bit her lip, her soul crying out, *Am I not to have a life of my own? Lord Jesus, isn't it enough to be a good servant, when once I was free?*

She heard a bench scrape, voices hushing, and then with sinking heart she visualized the scene taking place below. Goodman Amos had contrived to stay late, again. Zellaire had offered him the warmth of a pallet before the hearth, again. She heard Zellaire and her mother talking as they ascended the stairs.

Hurriedly she crept into the cold bed she shared with her mother and pretended to be asleep.

When Marie Therese climbed in beside her and felt her cold limbs, Gennie knew she had not been fooled. "Relax, *chérie*," Marie Therese whispered in a tired voice. "What is the matter now?"

"Just nothing!" she hissed.

"*Bien.* Then go to sleep."

"How can I sleep with that—that ogre downstairs?"

"*Ogre?* Gennie! Mr. Amos is Henri's guest. The trouble with you is that life's been too easy."

Gennie shot bolt upright. "How can you say that?"

"Only because you do not realize how fortunate we are," replied Marie Therese wearily. "If you had had a few harsh experiences growing up—something to make you understand, Gennie, how things could be so much worse. And you might mention that sometime in your prayers, instead of spending so much time on your knees complaining."

"I'm not complaining. I'm praying for Papa and Phillippe." Gennie flounced back down and pulled the coverlet around her ears.

Marie Therese reached around her stiff form and hugged her. "Pray for them. But remember what Sister Margarethe said."

Gennie didn't answer.

"It is up to us to go on living," Marie Therese said very softly.

Sometime in the middle of the night, Gennie reawakened and knew she had been crying. Terrible nightmares had robbed her of peaceful sleep. Gently she slid out of bed. Her teeth were chattering, and she tried to swallow the noisy hiccups. Her dreams were tangled in her consciousness as her long flannel nightie was still tangled in the bedclothes. She fumbled for her shoes and crept downstairs, pausing to pull them on over her bare feet. She wrapped her heavy shawl around her before gently lifting the latch on the heavy oak door.

Moonlight transformed the night into silver, with black paper cutouts for trees and stiles. Her breath formed little clouds. Ice crystals sparkled around the rim of the bucket at the well. Suddenly her body contracted in an uncontrollable shiver. She bent almost double and scurried for the barn, pulling the heavy door shut behind her, to close out the icy draught.

Gennie felt immediately safe in the inky barn. Its fecund odors soothed her racing mind, comforted her with remembrances of home. In confidence she moved in the blackness to burrow a little nest for herself in clean straw and listen to the familiar music of the animals. Suddenly a phrase came to mind that the Huguenot preacher had used last Sunday. "Cast all your anxieties on Him, for He cares about you."

Gennie sniffled and wiped her cheeks with the edge of her shawl, ordering her rebellious mind to be still and think about this. How lucky they were that M. Zellaire was a good and pious man and that in this province of Pennsylvania they were allowed to have their French Reformed Church. And how lucky . . . how lucky . . . determinedly she searched her mind . . . to have a warm and pretty dress. And to be wearing it when Thomas Roebuck came calling!

She smiled involuntarily, and then fresh tears sprang to her eyes. Yes, a handsome young man, a warrior like Charlemagne, but how could he help her? He was leaving soon, and an ugly old man was sniffing around, wanting a warm bed and soft new flesh to anchor his old bones to!

Gennie wrenched her mind from this paralyzing thought. *Papa and Phillippe. Sweet Lord Jesus, only you can do something about them. Only you know if they still live. Oh, I cannot bear it! Please take this fear, Lord. Take it!* Suddenly Gennie felt a stillness come upon her. A cleansing sense of release. Then came in place of her fear a rush of love for her mother, who buried her own griefs and needs so that she could devote herself to her daughter and now to the needs of this new family, which she seemed to embrace without resentment.

After all, does one blame the rescuer for the misfortunes that have gone before? God had sent them to a good man. And in his goodness, Henri Zellaire surely would not deliberately do something bad.

Lord, she decided, *I will go no further than that. In thee I have placed my trust.* Resolutely she shut Thomas Roebuck out of her mind. Such a silly girl, to dream that a free man, an officer fighting the Papists, cared for an indentured serving girl, beyond being kind and sympathetic to her.

Gennie climbed to her feet, shaking the clinging straw from her shawl. She would not think of him, and she would not think of the old man. She would stay her mind on her Lord and trust him for whatever came.

When Gennie let herself in the door of the house, her fingers fumbled numbly with the icy latch. Her teeth clattered so loudly she could not suppress a verbal shudder. She swallowed a wild urge to giggle.

A sleep-raw voice shot out of the darkness: "Who is that?"

"Only me! I—I forgot something." She fled up the stairs, fighting down the panic Goodman Amos' voice brought back, desperately clinging to her resolution of calm trust. Gennie twisted her hands together. To trust God amidst the safety of gentle farm animals was quite easier than when facing a frightful voice out of the night.

sap, *a stupid beggar, a poor ninny.* Thomas poised naked in the chilly air, his toes curling over the ridge of granite slab that jutted over the river. *A jackstraw fool!* he muttered as he dove into the freezing waters. He swam rapidly and skillfully for several minutes, relishing the agony of the water chastising his body. Zellaire had taken him in, all right, no less than the poltroon who had stolen his fur harvest.

Don't tell his price indeed! What Thomas had discovered was that when Zellaire thought he had the market cornered for the sale of military arms, he had, without conscience and without an iota of patriotism, overcharged him at least by half for the flintlocks. No wonder he did not want his price bandied. But he must have known his greed would surface.

Thomas was dead tired and saddle sore. He had ridden only Pa's mule before joining Wolcott's forces and was learning the hard way how to ride comfortably, sparing both himself and his horse, for days on end. He had pushed himself, knowing Wolcott was pressed for time and that the assault on Louisbourg was to take place as soon as the ice broke in the north.

He had spent the last four days making the rounds of gunsmiths. The entire valley north and south of Germantown and west of Philadelphia was dotted with independent craftsmen like Zellaire. Like a loosely structured guild, most knew the others: who was making what and how each man's work differed. Wolcott would get what he wanted: one hundred flintlock rifles delivered to Boston within three weeks. Not all their parts were interchangeable, but at least a fair degree of uniformity existed in the shot. It remained now to confront Henri Zellaire.

Refreshed by the brief swim, Thomas dressed hurriedly. He patted the pouch in place under his shirt before donning his greatcoat. Only a few pence left from his first month's wages. Perhaps Madame Harmonie would not take it amiss if he brought a trinket for Gennie.

It was raining when Thomas reined in before Goodman Amos' Mercantile. This time he would not tell Amos where he was heading, lest the garrulous old man discover reason to accompany him again.

The store appeared empty. From a curtained enclosure beyond

the long counter at the rear of the room, Thomas heard Amos and another man in animated conversation. Idly he sauntered around the
shop, eyeing laces and buttons among the dress goods; and at a far
end buckets, blankets, ropes of tobacco, knives, and tomahawks.

His eyes lighted on a dainty porcelain teacup and saucer, incon-
gruous among the sturdier items. Delicately painted daffodils adorned
the cup, which was so thin that when he held it toward the light he
could see the flowers silhouetted through the porcelain. It reminded
him of Gennie.

"I'll arrange everything, Goodman," said the man now coming
through the curtain. He was dressed in the garb of a sea captain.

"Good, good!" said Goodman Amos, following him into the
store. "How long—well young Roebuck!"

Thomas set the cup down gently. "Good morning, sir."

"Not long," the man said. "Couple months at most. Two husky
lads who can do a man's work. The man would be a fool not to agree
to the trade."

Amos shot a glance at Thomas. "Fine, fine. Well, fair winds to
ye." He turned his back abruptly to his associate, effectively cutting
off further conversation, and said to Thomas with a broad smile, "On
your way back to the war?"

"Yes, sir. I'll take this cup. Can you wrap it well?"

"Taking a teacup to war," said Amos, amused. "How times have
changed."

Ignoring the gibe, Thomas paid for the cup and left quickly.

A mood of depression settled on him, matching the rain. The
horse was fresh and threshed out the miles at a steady trot while he
wrestled with his feelings about Gennie.

Seven years. Could he wait seven years for a wife? Did he love
her enough for that? But surely something could be done! Yet was she
truly attracted to him, or did she want above all else to be free again?
He tried to imagine how she must feel, once as free as he, with her
whole life before her, and then to have a nameless, faceless power destroy nearly everything held dear. Now it was in the hands of Providence. And if God wanted Thomas and Gennie together, he would
show Thomas the way.

Thomas spurred the horse to move a little faster.

If Thomas had seen Gennie at this moment, he might have concluded it was a poor time to visit.

Gennie was wadding up her unbleached linsey-woolsey dress
against the sides of her hips as she confronted her mother. They had

been hanging wet clothes over lines strung before the hearth. The voices of the children playing upstairs drifted down.

"But I *have* to do what he says!" Gennie repeated.

"But he hasn't told you to do anything," Marie Therese said patiently. "I wish you would tell me what it is you think Henri will ask you to do."

A month had passsed since Gennie had spoken to Rosalind Hambleton on the porch of the mercantile. Since Thomas's last visit, the woman's shocking words had preyed upon her even more strongly. She awoke each morning, murmuring urgently, "In Christ is my refuge."

And during the day, Marie Therese would overhear her canting, "Thou will grant her perfect peace, whose mind is stayed on thee." Marie Therese had begun to be alarmed. Gennie did all she was asked, quickly and without complaint. But after chores, she no longer romped with the children on clear days outside, swinging them by the long rope tied up in the bare limbs of the maple tree or playing snowshoe tag or gathering cones.

This morning, Gennie had seemed particularly agitated. "You are ruining your dress, pulling it that way," her mother said. "Why are you doing that!"

"Because I am nothing!" Gennie flung at her. She burst into sobs.

"*Chérie, chérie* . . ." Marie Therese parted the lines of wet clothing and gathered Gennie to her as if she were still a child. "What brought this on? Come, sit with me." Marie Therese pulled her down on the braided rug before the warm fire and cradled her. "There, there," she crooned. "Nobody can harm you. Mama's here. Tell Mama all about it."

So Gennie blurted the truth about Rosalind Hambleton. "And Mama," she said at last, "I just know that Rosalind was talking about herself when she said a master can come into your bed any old time he wants to! It must have happened to her!" Again she was off in broken sobs. "And—and Mama, if it can happen to Rosalind, it can happen to you! Or me! Or M. Zellaire can sell us. He has the right!"

They rocked for several minutes, Marie Therese patting back the damp locks, smoothing Gennie's dress over her ankles, doing the little things that mothers have done always, meaningless gestures, yet powerful transmitters of love.

"Do you remember when we were in the convent, trying to understand how someone could be so evil as to take away Papa and Phillippe and destroy our farm? Do you remember what we decided?"

Gennie nodded. "Somebody wanted our farm, and they didn't care about us at all; they just wanted what we had."

"And . . ."

"And maybe they said it was because we were not Catholics, but that was not it at all; it was just the excuse."

Marie Therese nodded, continuing to rock Gennie there on the floor. "We knew that because we had friends and family who were also Catholics, and we still loved each other."

"Yes, but—"

"Sometimes there are bad men, Gennie. If it happens that some poor girl comes into their grasp, then, God help us, they turn their nature against God; instead of fighting that nature they give in. And just the way the bad people who stole our farm told themselves they were righteous because we were Protestants, so it is that men who do other terrible things tell themselves it is honorable, because they own the other person."

"And M. Zellaire owns us!" Gennie's voice unraveled with a fear that was now out in the open.

"*Chérie*, you have not heard. Only a few would steal a farm, and only a few would take advantage of helpless women. Our Savior has delivered us here safely. You must trust him. . . . Perhaps the best you and I can do now is to secure the love of a good man," Marie Therese said slowly. "Then he will be our protector against any who would harm us."

Warm thoughts of Thomas rushed into Gennie's mind. "But what about Papa?"

Marie Therese did not answer right away. "We have to trust God. And trust also that he is overseeing the lives of those around us," she amended firmly. She felt Gennie relax. Knowing Gennie, she would probably have to mull all this over in her mind before they spoke of it again. Marie Therese hugged her. "Know what?"

"What?"

"If we do not get the rest of these clothes up, no one will have dry linens for church tomorrow."

Gennie scrambled to her feet and reached to help her mother up. "Oh, Mama, I love you!"

As the two women stood smiling at each other, the door burst open. "Gennie! Gennie! Thomas Roebuck is here, and he's come to see *you*. Are you courtin'?"

"Jean Zellaire, what were you doing out in the rain?" Jean's clothes were soaked and muddy, his cheeks as appealingly red as frosted plums. Thomas was only a step behind.

"Mr. Roebuck!" Hastily Gennie brushed at her eyes with the back of her hand and tugged at her wrinkled dress. "We weren't expecting you!" Her eyes sparkled under tear-wet lashes.

Thomas smiled down at her radiant face. "I could not stay away, Gennie, and that's the truth."

"Praise be," Marie Therese murmured under her breath.

"Come in. Oh! All these clothes! Let me take your wet things. There is still room to hang them by the fire." Gennie rushed about, whipping wet wash off one line, directing Jean to take Thomas's oilskins out to the porch to drip.

Pandemonium reigned for several minutes. The other three children heard Jean's excited voice and exploded down the stairs. Marie Therese bribed them with Indian bread to play upstairs a while longer.

Gennie gazed up at Thomas. He smelled of wet wool. Standing here, so big, in the middle of the room, his eyes glowing softly, she felt his love reach out and envelop her. She shivered.

"Ye look a little teary eyed. Not catching a cold, are ye?"

"I am fine, Mr. Roebuck. Thank you." Her smile was dazzling.

Why did he think the effort cost her so much? Once again he had the impression that she was caught in a web of violent emotions. "I brought you a gift. A silly one, maybe." Carefully he produced the string-wrapped package.

Gennie's eyes shone with anticipation as she opened it. Her fingers trembled as she placed cup on saucer with a gentle *clink*. "Oh, Mr. Roebuck. It is so beautiful and so delicate. Look, Mama." Suddenly she giggled. "How did you manage to get it here without breaking it?"

He grinned. "No one can be a clod all the time."

"I didn't mean . . ." Gennie blushed and glanced at her mother.

With an effort, Thomas tore himself away. He, too, glanced at Marie Therese.

"Where is Mr. Zellaire?"

"In the workshop," Marie Therese answered.

Thomas's gaze bore into Gennie. "Don't go away," he whispered huskily. Then he strode purposefully across the room. The door opened suddenly, and Zellaire met him in the doorway, wearing a leather apron.

The good-natured, freckled face underwent a change of expression, from habitual conviviality, to recollection, and then to obstinacy as he saw Thomas's face.

"May we talk?"

"Certainly. Come in the workshop."

Thomas lost no time coming to the heart of the matter. He threw down his gloves on Zellaire's cold forge. "It was no accident, was it, that you directed me to the Crown and Rose? You knew that General Wolcott was headquartered there and that your friend the tavern keeper could be counted upon to see that Wolcott received a demonstration of your flintlock."

A look of chagrin crossed Zellaire's features. "So? You must admit he fancied the gun quite as much as you!"

When in doubt, attack. Thomas studied the self-righteous face, then let out an exasperated whistle. "How nice that you are such a patriot."

"I did tell you where to get the rest of your guns."

"So you did." Blast the man! Thomas felt so inexpert. An officer in the militia ought to command respect! Yet all he felt was his youth and the certainty of his love for Gennie. Goodman Amos had taken the initiative away from him on his last visit. Was Zellaire now to gloat that he had "put one over on him," taking advantage of his inexperience, to make money? He loved Gennie. Seeing her face so dewy and alive when he came in convinced him that she loved him, too. It was not fair that she should have to serve this man seven years for a wrong she had never been part of!

Thomas found that he was praying fervently for the lever to pry loose Zellaire's atrophied sense of Christian humanity. Suddenly the inspiration he had been seeking came.

"Yes. I am sorry now to tell you that the militia governments may have to buy in the future from the others when they realize the difference in price. And the quality," Thomas shot a glance at Zellaire, feeling stronger as he went along, "while perhaps not *quite* as fine as yours, is almost so."

"Not quite? Nowhere near!" Zellaire sputtered.

Thomas began to pace, using his fingers to help him calculate some figures. "According to my estimate, you made a profit almost equal to one passage from England to Boston." He turned to face Zellaire, who by now seemed most uncomfortable.

"Gennie's passage, for example. But what a wonderful thing, since the Quakers—the neighbors I recall you said you admire so much? and respect?—yes, those whose business you desire, who frown upon slavery in any form, will certainly realize what a fine Christian fellow you must be to rescue a poor young Huguenot."

"Now, wait, Thomas. What has this to do with . . . ?"

Thomas plunged recklessly on. "And allow her to make her own choice, as God would have it, and to become betrothed to a young man of good character who would always love and respect you as a dutiful son should."

Five minutes passed. Assorted snorts and exhalations punctuated the battle within the wily Zellaire. Finally he sat heavily on an upended stump of wood.

"To tell you truthfully, Thomas, my conscience is torn hither and yon by the whole affair. I, too, am in love, lad, and unable to do anything about it." He smiled ruefully. "For a while I fooled myself. Goodman Amos suggested I sell Gennie to him. It was a most attractive trade!" he said with a shade of regret.

Thomas blanched and turned a few paces away from Henri.

"He quite convinced me that with Gennie gone, her mother would willingly share my bed, marriage or no. But not Marie Therese! Were I to so much as ask her I would lose her—not as a servant: She will be faithful till the last of her days with me—but as a mate in God's holy sight. Even if we could learn with certainty her husband's fate."

Filled with righteous indignation and prepared to foil Henri by any means, Thomas was unprepared for the blurted confession. Suddenly he felt their kinship, both wanting the same—a mate to love and be loved by.

Awkwardly he touched Henri's shoulder. "Isn't there any way to find out if Monsieur Harmonie lives?"

Zellaire shook his head. "A Sister Margarethe at the convent in Le Havre believes he is dead—and the little boy, Phillippe; none who have been so treated have ever again been seen. Yet without proof, Marie Therese risks eternal damnation were she to take another husband."

He gave a morose shrug. "I could tell her that I had discovered proof her husband is dead. I know she cares for me. I know she is lonely. I hear her crying sometimes late at night. I long to comfort her. But a man cannot risk the horrors of hell. Not for her, not for myself. For I would be equally guilty."

Unbidden, Thomas's mind began racing with the dawning possibility that Zellaire intended to let Gennie go. If she would have him!

"Mr. Zellaire, I have no money or property yet, but if you will consent to let Gennie marry me after this war, I will repay you yearly, with furs, until her contract is paid off. And after all, what is she to you but another mouth to feed? Her mother is as capable as a mother could be with your family, and you really do not need another pair of girl's hands in the business in which you are engaged."

"Furs, heh?" Zellaire kneaded his lower lip. "I suppose I did trick you into showing my flintlock to General Wolcott and thereby profited."

"Aye, that you did," Thomas agreed, holding his breath, not daring to interrupt the thoughts he fancied spinning behind that burnt-freckles exterior.

"And guns for the war, if more are needed?"

Thomas hesitated. He shook his head. "You will have to take your chances with the others."

Zellaire grinned. It was worth a try. "All right, lad. Permission to speak to Gennie. And should she agree, why, after the war we will have the finest wedding ever seen in Germantown."

Thomas leaped in the air, emitting an ear-splitting Indian yell.

·C·H·A·P·T·E·R· **14** ·

homas and Gennie escaped from the stifling snugness of the house into a world at peace. Water dripped off branches of dark and sodden oaks. The earth seemed to have exhausted itself with the end of the rainstorm and now waited, silently regathering strength.

Thomas frowned in concentration, his eyes fixed on choosing a secure path. As they walked, he tucked Gennie's hand, as if by habit, in the woolly warmth between arm and chest. Elated by his success with Zellaire, he realized he did not know if Gennie loved him.

Gennie let her hand be taken and followed his path. Her face was troubled, if he had cared to look. Her heart ached for him and for herself, if he had cared to question. How confident he seemed. How little he knew!

"Gennie?" Thomas halted.

"Yes, Mr. Roebuck."

"You didn't answer my question."

"What question, Mr. Roebuck?"

"About, well, you know—do you—do you like me well enough to—when you get to know me better, could I . . ." In disgust Thomas kicked at a clod of earth and ice, lobbing it into a field. Something rustled in the weeds as it landed, a quick scurry, then silence again.

"I am not free to think about you."

"You are, Gennie. I spoke to Mr. Zellaire. He is willing to let me—" *buy your contract*, he started to say. But the words seemed heartless, as if she were no more than chattel. ". . . to let us marry, if you will have me, after the war."

To his astonishment, she blurted, "Why would he do that?"

"Because I told him I love you," he said quietly.

"He would never . . . it isn't like him!"

"He is in love with your mother."

Gennie just stared at him, as if she had been seeing nothing but her own dark fears for so long that she could not comprehend her swift change of fortune.

"By thunder, Gennie, ye behave as if you cannot trust Christ himself!"

Gennie gasped. "In Christ is my only refuge. In him alone since

79

Papa and Phillippe were taken away! There is no safety anywhere else!"

"Pshaw! Christ loves me, too, ye know! Don't ye think it possible that he might want to entrust you to me? What need does he have of you the way a man does?"

"Oh! Oh!"

"God wants you to behave as a woman, Gennie Harmonie, not some—some stone statue!"

She tried to cover her face and ears.

Thomas seized her wrists and forced them to her sides.

"All I ever wanted was to stay home, to live in my own home with my family!" The cords in her neck stood out as she trembled before him, her face contorted with agony, tears sheeting from eyelids squeezed tightly together.

"If you trust in God, girl, show it! Give him credit for knowing what you need! How can God work in our lives if not through others? Gennie, Gennie, I'm going to build that home for you! Providence willing, it will be all yours, little Gen, yours and mine and our children's."

Gennie's eyes opened. She hiccupped and looked up at Thomas, her lips parted slightly. "Y-you, Mr. Roebuck?"

Thomas yelped with laughter and threw his arms around her, picking her off her feet and jigging up and down. " 'You, Mr. Roebuck?' Yes, me, Mr. Roebuck! Who do you think? Doesn't God want the best for you, Gennie? And that's me! Oh, yeah, that's me! Gennie . . ."

She stood very still in the circle of his arms. Slowly her face lifted to his. He felt the tension leave her body and her arms creep tentatively around his back. Tenderly he bent his lips to hers. Suddenly her arms tightened and she was answering his kiss with her own.

———————◆•◆———————

"But Mama always told me," Gennie was saying a little later as they sat on the stone stile, munching early strawberries, "to seek a man who would protect me. I just thought she meant someone rich and strong enough to keep me from harm in life."

"You were trying to protect the wrong thing. You trust Providence, you live life, and God protects you—from yourself, most likely," he grinned.

She smiled shyly.

Thomas felt very virtuous and extremely philosophical, certainly years older in experience than this naive, appealing French girl. Why, she couldn't weigh more than a good-sized pumpkin! How could a girl so tiny even have his babies?

Gennie glanced over at him. "Mr. Roebuck," she said in alarm, "what is the matter? Are you ill? Have you eaten too many green berries? Oh, dear . . ."

He felt himself grow warm. "Sweet one, I was never better." He looked at the berries left in his hand and tossed them into the weeds. He looked at hers. Under the berries, Gennie's hand was stained scarlet. For an instant it appeared to him drenched in blood. He felt a moment of sickening, hollow fear in the pit of his stomach. Swiftly he wiped their palms with his kerchief and lifted her down from the stile. "Oh, Gennie. I do love you. . . . Do you love me?"

"Yes, Mr. Roebuck—Thomas. Thomas," she repeated, a note of wonder in her voice. "Oh, yes, Thomas, I do love you!"

A strange, unsettling thought came to him as she slipped her hand in his: Did she love him, Thomas Roebuck, or did she love knowing that at last she had found a protector?"

As if she had read his mind, Gennie stopped. She took his rangy hands, put them together, and cupped them in her small ones. "I'll take such good care of you, Thomas," she promised. "Come back to me safely."

"Oh, Gennie. What a wonderful life we'll have!"

His spirits had soared as he bade final farewell to Gennie and her mother and the Zellaires and rode for Philadelphia, where he would catch the coach for Boston.

With time to spare, he waited on the porch of the hotel in Philadelphia, watching the coach being loaded.

"Sandy McGinnis, isn't it?"

"Aye, sir. Excuse me, sir. Step lively, lads, we haven't all day!" McGinnis's long jaw jutted forward as he barked commands to two men, one heaving baggage to the other atop McGinnis's coach.

"Tell me, Mr. McGinnis, are we stopping at the Croaking Crow this trip?" Thomas called.

"That's a regular stop," McGinnis answered, not diverting his attention from the sweating workers.

Thomas sauntered over to read the notices posted outside the double doors of the Philadelphia hotel. Rewards were posted for runaway slaves and indentured servants. A crudely lettered sign offered to TRACKE YE RUNAGATES AND RETURN THEM TO THEIR LAWFULLE OWNERS. In a slot under the notices was a weekly newspaper, published at the hotel, with a neat note imploring gentlemen who were learning to read to please use last week's paper.

"It seems you have taken this coach before," said a low voice at his ear. Thomas turned. The speaker was man about thirty, garbed in a sober black suit.

"Yes. You a passenger?"

"Not this trip. Tell me, sir, the last time you stopped at the Croaking Crow, did a parson appear out of nowhere, and by the time his blessing was finished and the meal served, did McGinnis insist on taking off again?"

"Yes! How did you . . . ?"

"A stableyard understanding, no doubt." The man's eyes crinkled in a wry smile. "Between the coachman and Mrs. Puddister. She owns the tavern. For while we were brushing the dust from our clothes, mustering, and saying grace, McGinnis was eating and drinking as fast as he could, and I did not observe that he paid anything."

"Yes, it was the same with us!"

"I have it on reliable authority that the so-called parson is a ne'er-do-well brother of the Puddister person."

"God's truth?"

"God's truth. A pleasant journey to you." The man hooked his thumbs in his waistcoat and gave Thomas a tongue-in-cheek smile before strolling on.

Thomas stared after him and then at McGinnis. The foul trickery of the man! Perhaps two could play at that game.

Thomas laid aside thoughts of McGinnis as the coach got under way and thought ahead to Boston. The Connecticut regiment would already be rendezvousing with American and British troops from the other provinces who had agreed to join the war against the French.

With God's grace they would banish French ships from American fishing grounds, then take Louisbourg and drive them back to Quebec. Thomas closed his eyes, feeling the sway and jolt of the coach. . . . He was on the crest of a hill urging his men onward, the French fleeing in disarray from the deadly accuracy of their flintlocks. . . . His hand moved unconsciously to his breast, where, tucked in an inside pocket, lay the agreements for the rifles.

Hours later, as if the devil were behind it, the coach whirled into the yard of the Croaking Crow tavern.

"Twenty minutes!" called Sandy McGinnis. "Twenty minutes!" He was off the high seat and gone before the last of the passengers had lumbered down.

Again, the "parson" appeared while they all sat at table. The driver was served his meal off in a corner and paid no attention whatever to the extended blessing. Thomas eyed the finely wrought silver spoons laid along the table. More than one man's hand inched toward his utensil, while the steam slowly disappeared from their victuals and the parson droned on.

Again, no one had consumed more than a bite before the driver leaped to his feet and demanded that all must leave. The passengers howled in hungry outrage, though they went. Thomas kept to his plate. Mrs. Puddister stared at him with a quizzical expression of her dough-round face before disappearing into the kitchen.

Thomas heard the coach leave. When he finished his last course, he called for a bowl of bread and milk for dessert. Mrs. Puddister served it herself. Thomas smiled his thanks. "Oh, and a spoon, if you please."

Mrs. Puddister looked around sharply. Of the unused silver spoons, kept in a pewter cup at each end of the table, not one remained. With an exclamation, she darted into the kitchen, reappearing only seconds later, bearing him a dented pewter spoon.

"Perhaps one of the passengers did not fancy going away without something for his money."

Mrs. Puddister's little raisin eyes stared at him. Then anger chased away her puzzled expression. With an unladylike curse, she hastened out the door.

Thomas heard her call one of the stable lads. Moments later a horse was heard to dash away. Leisurely Thomas finished his dessert and moved over to the fire. He propped his boots on the grate and began to pick his teeth. Soon a rattle of hooves and harnesses brought Mrs. Puddister rushing to the door.

She shook a finger at Thomas. "You just point out the man that took them spoons, sir!"

"Certainly, madam," Thomas rose and collected his coat. "I'll point him out. I took them myself. They are all in the big coffee pot on the end of the table."

Thomas stepped outside. He paused, getting into the coach. "Hurry up, McGinnis. I've had my dinner."

homas reached Boston in great spirits, eager now to cover himself with glory against the French and return to his love. For surely God was on their side. In every town he passed, from every pulpit, parsons were thundering against the Papists, whipping people into the belief they were fighting a holy war.

He found the new encampment with little difficulty, with the aid of a well-informed citizen. A wide, well-trampled path led from the outskirts of Boston to a spacious meadow ringed with trees in full leaf of spring. Rows of uniform white tents defined the British presence. The bulk of the grounds sported tents of every earthy hue and form, interspersed with an occasional jerry-built cabin.

Peter Sparhawk was nowhere around when Thomas reached the officers' section. Private Billy Lang, their steward, was sitting, unshaven and bleary eyed, on a stool inside the tent shared by Roebuck and Sparhawk. Billy was a runty man of close to sixty years, a native of Hartford, who had insisted on volunteering "to go to war."

" 'Morning, Billy. Where is Lieutenant Sparhawk?"

Billy stared up at him, his lower lip quivering petulantly. "Not going." The pungent odor of rum arose from Billy.

"Not going? Who is not going?"

"Me, sir."

Thomas pulled a campstool over in front of the man and sat. "Are you ill?"

"It's me missus, sir." Billy did not meet his eyes. When Thomas didn't respond, he shot him a quick glance. "It's the little ones. Them bein' sick an' all." Billy's mouth worked like a cow's chewing cud. Finally he raised a flask and swallowed deeply, his Adam's apple moving rhythmically up and down.

Thomas waited, trying to keep disapproval off his face, recalling Wolcott's admonition that the men's presence was voluntary. He wasn't sure Billy's presence was worth the effort.

"I did not know your family was ill, Billy."

"Oh, yessir!" Billy brightened. For the next few minutes he embellished his tale, while Thomas tried to read between the lines. He had met Billy's "missus" before leaving Hartford, a work-toughened woman who had been widowed with two half-grown children at the time she married Billy. All were hale then. ". . . an' who's to care for them tykes if I was took?" Ah. Now he could read in part the pleading in Billy's eyes. Billy doted on his "missus," certain that every man envied him his good fortune in marrying her. And who would care for his family if he was "took"?

"Most of the men have families, Billy. Don't you trust Providence to bring you safely home again?"

" 'Spose so, sir."

"I imagine your missus is very proud of you."

" 'Spose so, sir?"

"Indeed. And I'll take care of you, Billy. That is a promise."

Billy's eyes strayed to the flask held loosely in one hand, as if this promise beckoned more brightly.

"Have you seen Lieutenant Sparhawk?"

"Left you a message, he did, sir. Says if you was to come back today, you was to join him an' the gen'rul at the Bowl and Three Spoons."

"Is there a horse about I can use?"

"One o' them fancy pacers, I 'spose. I'll get him saddled up."

"I'll do it, Billy. You write to your missus. It will make you feel better. And shuck that flask. You need your wits about you."

The Bowl and Three Spoons tavern was a pink brick building occupying a prominent place across the street from Boston Common. Thomas was ushered to the second floor.

Hearing voices in vigorous debate beyond the door, he entered discreetly. He was in a spacious, oak-beamed room that ran the length of the building. Paneled fireplaces at either end filled the air with warmth and the aroma of hickory smoke, mingling with the fragrance of tobacco smoke that drifted over the room like vapor.

A table had been set up on the polished, bare floor, in the center of the room. Clustered around it were a score of men, few of whom he knew. He could see no British officers.

Roger Wolcott glanced around at him, his aquiline, intelligent face breaking into a brief smile of welcome, but not inviting immediate entry into the discussion. Thomas noted with approval Wolcott's well-cut wine broadcloth coat and new white trousers. His stock was modestly devoid of lace, but his expensive brown boots shone from a vigorous spit and polish.

From the far side of the room, Peter Sparhawk nodded to him, one thumb stroking his luxuriant black moustache as he stood among several other junior officers. Thomas heard a familiar voice and moved slightly to catch sight of the speaker.

It was Nathaniel Sparhawk, Peter's father. Sparhawk had the bull head, thick neck, and shoulders of a man who had spent his youth at tough labor, as if he had personally wrestled his immense fortune from the whales, before turning his ships to privateering. He was now a captain in the Massachusetts contingent.

Thomas had spent a night in the Sparhawk mansion in Boston and recalled a staff of servants peforming tasks that occupied his mother endlessly—spinning, weaving, making cheese and butter. Whale oil was used in place of the cheaper and poor-quality tallow candles of his father's house. He had admired the rich, dark woods, felt the cool, polished balustrades and plate rails, the shelves that displayed relics of Sparhawk's years as a whaler.

"We ought to let George and Louis tear each other's crowns off and keep our hands clean," grumbled Nathaniel Sparhawk.

No one answered him, and Thomas's attention was captured by a short, stocky man with vigorous gestures. His ruddy face was that of a peaceable man, with eyes that gazed at the others with an air of confidence and trust. Without appearing to do so, he dominated the gathering. Thomas was willing to bet the man was William Pepperrell, of Massachusetts.

Massachusetts, supplying over three thousand men and subsidizing hundreds more who came from other colonies, had claimed the right to name a commander-in-chief of the American forces. It had not been easy to persuade individual colonies to agree upon a single commander.

"Our letters to King George and the duke of Marlborough have yet to be answered," Pepperrell was saying. "While we wait, we must place our faith in Providence and proceed on our own. What is our naval strength?"

Sparhawk spoke first for Massachusetts. "Sir, we found a brig on the stocks nearly ready for launching. She's been converted to a frigate mounted with twenty-four guns and named the *Massachusetts*. We have two with twenty guns; two with sixteen, including the *Boston Packet*; a sloop of twelve; and two of eight."

Other colonies added their contributions.

"Two French men-of-war would outmatch our whole navy," observed Sparhawk. "General Pepperrell, I happen to know that Commodore Peter Warren of His Majesty's navy is now with a small squadron at Antigua, doing some—er—business on the side. I suggest we express a boat to him, with a letter stating the situation and asking his aid."

"Would he help without letters from the king?"

"Warren is married to an American. She has considerable property on the Mohawk. He is sympathetic to the colonies and has his own interests to protect."

"By all means, Nathaniel, let us contact the man." Pepperrell turned to Roger Wolcott. "Now about our land forces."

Wolcott generously allowed Thomas to hold forth on the virtues of the new flintlock. When he had finished, Pepperrell turned the full force of his approving smile upon him. Thomas experienced such a flow of warmth he knew he would follow Pepperrell wherever he was told to go.

Talk returned to a general discussion of the best way to contain the French.

A huge, powerful-looking man clad in a loose-fitting coat of homespun undyed wool said thoughtfully, "Whoever gains control of the Ohio will win. If we take it, we cut New France in half. If they take it, they crowd us back to the sea."

"That is true, Colonel Butler," agreed a sea captain, now wearing the insignia of major. "But it does no good to sack a French post or two on the Ohio if ships can sail as free as you please up the Saint Lawrence to Quebec. Take out their fortress at Louisbourg, and you control the sea lanes. And their only means of keeping those forts on the Ohio supplied."

"I agree," said another. "Louisbourg is too powerful to bypass."

"After Louisbourg, then what?" demanded Nathaniel Sparhawk, then answered himself: "I'll tell ye what: No more brandy, that is what. No more fancy goods for the ladies. And we'll pay a greater tariff on things from home. We were not doing badly as privateers."

Thomas smiled. Peter had told him that his father was still smarting under the government's edict that the *Sparhawk* and all other so-called fishing vessels in Boston Harbor must be fitted out as ships of war for the duration of the fighting.

Sparhawk thrust his bull head into the glare of the chandelier. "I agree with the colonel. Concentrate our efforts on chasing the French out of the Ohio valley. They are not strong enough to defend both frontiers."

"Neither are we," said Wolcott.

"So let the French keep their fishing fleet and we our privateers. We steal back more than they make in fish!"

Sparhawk's audacious jest was met by a ripple of laughter; then broadsided by a sharp rap at the door. Standing nearest the door, Thomas opened it. He accepted a thick paper packet from the messenger. It was addressed to General William Pepperrell.

Pepperrell broke the blob of red sealing wax and scanned the letter. He glanced around the room. "The French have taken Canseau."

Thomas caught Peter Sparhawk's eye across the room. Action at last!

"By gar, that tears it, it does!" exploded the sea-captain major. "If it is war they want, 'tis war they shall have!"

Canseau was an English fishing village perched on the rim of the Grand Banks fishing grounds, only fifty miles south of Louisbourg.

A move against an established colony meant only one thing: The French were moving out of the fish-and-run tactics of a harassment operation and headed for conquest. Now the Americans dare not divert attention to the Ohio. Their colonies themselves were in danger.

"I have been to Cape Breton Island," mused Nathaniel Sparhawk. "Not to the fort itself, of course, that is built on the northern end. But I've seen it. Bedded in fogs as thick as chowder. In winter the drifts reach as high as the ramparts."

"That run of coast eats ships—"

"I don't pretend to be a military man," Pepperrell confessed. "Nothing makes me fit to lay siege to Louisbourg. Yet the French have made our decision for us, and this is what we must do. We have not one officer of experience, nor even an engineer, to tell us how to go about it." Pepperrell's gaze swept his officers.

In the silence Thomas could hear the quiet, comforting crackle of the fires.

"By all that is sacred, gentlemen, we must pray for divine guidance if we are to come out of this whole."

·C·H·A·P·T·E·R· **16** ·

he regiments threw themselves into preparations for the siege of Louisbourg. As the new flintlocks arrived Thomas drove his men in continuous drills. The day before they were to board for Canseau, Wolcott ordered eight hours leave for everyone, with admonitions to stay in groups and not to go about unarmed.

For the past week reports had filtered in of sightings of Mohican hunting parties. Mohicans did not usually venture this far into English lands, especially since their enemies the Iroquois abounded in the hills and valleys overlooking Boston.

"Which leads me to think," Wolcott had told his officers last evening, "that some of the men are not Mohican but French spies, got up as natives."

Without the presence of the sharpshooters on the rifle range, the camp was so quiet Thomas could hear birds calling back and forth and spot the sudden flutter of leaves. Nest building seemed in full swing.

Thomas stretched his booted legs out before him. He was sitting in a pool of sunlight, on a campstool outside his tent. He could hear Billy Lang inside, whistling through his teeth as he packed gear for the move. Billy had declined to use his leave, since he was "too far from the missus anyway." After his earlier bout of alcohol-induced self-pity, Lang had been an exemplary steward. Neither he nor Thomas had mentioned the episode again.

Thomas caressed the letter in his lap. Gennie had received his letter. Zellaire had translated it for her. He smiled tenderly. Gennie was determined to learn to read and write English, as well as to speak it. Her letter read like a primer of simple sentences: *My dear Mr. Roebuck, How are you? I am fine. M. Zellaire is help me with the words hards. When you come home I will write very good. Yr. obed. & faithfull servant, Gennie Harmonie.*

Not a typical love letter, but then, he could picture Gennie, in her modesty, with Zellaire instructing over her shoulder. He had answered Gennie's letter last night, certain that the love that warmed his heart was returned, if she could but express herself freely. Thomas sighed. His thoughts turned to his parents.

Though it was unlikely many of them would be killed—and not

91

himself to be sure—he was of a mind to let them know that if God decided to take him as a young man, they should know that he was appreciative of the home they had given him for eighteen years. He eased himself off the campstool and went inside to fetch his writing case.

Honour'd Sir & Madame, he began. But his heart sang with Gennie! Though he had never attempted it, he felt like composing poetry. He scowled. First the letter a dutiful son owed his family. He wrote for several minutes. . . . *so by the time this reaches you, we shall be handing the French the drubbing they deserve*. . . .

"Hey, Roebuck!"

Thomas answered without looking up. "Hm?"

Peter Sparhawk leaned in the tent flap. "Let's go fishing." He had abandoned his coat. His full, white sleeves were rolled back to the elbow. "I've a mind to have Billy cook us a fresh whitefish for supper. And look."

With a conspiratorial grin he produced a bottle of pale French wine.

"Leave it to you! Where did you get it?"

"Father sent it. Who are you writing to?"

"My parents. My mother wrote that she's met Gennie and likes her. She says Gennie cannot believe her good fortune—"

"What conceit, my man!"

"No, you dolt. She expected to serve out her indenture, the full seven years. Now, when I come back, she will be free to marry."

"Oh. What changed her master's mind?"

Thomas grinned. "A little matter of business, a little matter of love. Providence."

"Your letter can wait. Let's go fishing."

Seeing he would get no more done anyway, with his exuberant friend around, Thomas good-naturedly laid aside his quill and corked the ink. He folded the unfinished letter and tucked it in its envelope inside his coat.

"Too warm for that," Peter said.

Thomas removed the coat and hung it carefully on a peg. "We'll be back in a couple hours, Billy."

"Right, sir," said the industrious steward.

It was a glorious, golden afternoon, warm for early summer, without humidity or insects. Using tadpoles as bait, the men cast their lines and were soon caught in the thrall of the peaceful afternoon. Thomas was imbued with a sense of waiting, of relishing what lay ahead, savoring the thought of adventure, yet not wanting to hurry it.

"What are you going to do when this is over?"

"My father wants me to follow him to sea."

"A whaler? But here you are in the artillery."

Peter chuckled and cast into the stream. "He also wanted me to volunteer with him, here in Boston."

"So you went to Hartford instead and volunteered under Wolcott."

"Well? So did you."

"Pennsylvania isn't officially at war. I had to go somewhere."

"Going back after?"

"Well I like farming . . ." Thomas fell silent. "I've never realized it before, but I don't exactly get along with my father. He is a good man, but, well, now that I have met men like Roger Wolcott and your father and some of the others, I see that not all are like him. So— so—not strict exactly, but not open. My father is interested first in his farm, and next in absolute, unquestioning obedience from us. That includes my mother. Obedience from her. I don't want my wife to be like that."

My wife. He smiled, thinking of Gennie. She often acted frightened, dependent. But in her fierce love for her personal Christ he sensed a strength that she herself was not aware of yet. A frown knitted his black eyebrows. *There'll be no fear in our family!* he thought.

"When I get back, I'm going to take Gennie west, if she's willing. Into the Ohio territory. I wrote to her about it. Peter—what about it? Wouldn't you like to go west? Come with us!"

"And be a farmer? Not me! I've no desire to leave Boston. After this is over, I probably will become a whaler."

"But then why—"

"Be a landlubber now? Purely for adventure!"

Thomas burst out laughing.

It was late afternoon, and the camp was coming alive before they headed back to their tent. Cookfires appeared here and there along the crisscross of muddy paths.

Where the news that they were embarking for Canseau had originally brought cheers and raucous jokes, now the mood, with afternoon spent, energies at low ebb, turned reflective. Half a dozen of the enlisted men gathered around Parson Moody, Wolcott's chaplain. Others talked in groups of two or three. No one seemed to want to be alone.

When they reached their tent, they found no lamp lighted and no cooking fire started.

"No Billy-boy," said Sparhawk, dropping the string of fish outside the door.

Thomas lighted the lamp and gave the tent a quick survey. "I wonder if Billy decided to drown himself in rum again." Roebuck had told Sparhawk of their aide's behavior.

"He's probably sleeping somewhere, and we'll have to cook our own supper."

"Well, I'll be!" Thomas burst out. "My new coat is gone!" He looked ruefully at Peter, feeling bereft and betrayed. "When we find Billy, ten to one we find my coat. I hope he doesn't get it muddied. That coat was the finest thing I ever owned. . . . Maybe I was too proud of it."

"Quit moaning, it was just a coat! You want to clean fish or peel potatoes?"

———————◆———————

Private Billy Lang did not return during the night. Maybe he had gone over the hill, back to his "missus." Roebuck scanned the faces of the men mustered along the docks to board the *Boston Packet*. The sea was running a strong current. Sunlight weakened by fog reflected off its steely gray waters. Another man had been reported missing, too, known to be Billy's frequent companion, with a similar taste for rum.

The men of their batteries filed past Roebuck and Peter Sparhawk. Thomas's heart brimmed with affection for them. It seemed impossible that a few months ago he had not known any of them. He threw Peter a confident smile, his blue eyes glinting with eagerness. The French might be able to steal farms from poor helpless families, but by all that was holy, that was a far cry from impudently seizing whole villages.

The gulls keened and swooped over the quay as the ships, cargoed to the waterline with troops, hoisted sail one by one, tipped graceful homage to the wind, and sailed out of Boston Harbor.

How far away Gennie seemed now, with her concern for her own farm, her passionate aversion to adventure. Well, he supposed it was only men who thirsted for excitement. Women, as was right, stayed home, where it was peaceful, and reared children.

"Wasn't it on the *Packet* that your Gennie sailed to America?" Sparhawk said.

It was as if Sparhawk had read his mind. He smiled. "I had forgotten."

"French, right?"

"Yes, Huguenot."

"How did she happen to arrive on an English ship?"

"I thought you knew." Thomas repeated the tragedy that had befallen Gennie's family.

Peter uttered a soft exclamation. "No wonder she wants no part of war."

Thomas glanced at his friend in surprise. He was right. How could he, Thomas, have been so stupid? Gennie'd had enough of violence and death to last a lifetime.

He rammed his hands in the pockets of his ill-fitting coat. A pox on that Billy. His coat had not turned up either.

·C·H·A·P·T·E·R· 17 ·

he trapper squatted on the downed log. He scratched at his painted chest. The dried slashes of red and blue paint pulled the hairs of the skin and itched madly. He listened as bird songs hesitantly, then more boldly, came back to the meadow where minutes before shrieks of anguish had mingled with howls of triumph.

His lip curled in repulsion as he watched his Indian comrades leisurely finish off the victims of their ambush. A scalp lifted here, a pocket watch, a pipe there, bringing delighted expressions.

He hated this war. He was a coureur de bois, not a war maker. *Nor a widow maker*, he thought, watching Chief Abinakis amble in his direction, wearing a gaudy green wool coat decorated with gold buttons. Still warm from the back of some Englishman, no doubt.

The French government paid their Indian allies to partake in raiding parties against the English. French and Indian alike painted their bodies and took scalps, a bloody custom introduced by the French a century ago, when they traded the tribes knives of steel to replace stone tomahawks. Having their Indian brothers take scalps they needn't account for bodies. It meant simplified bookkeeping no end.

Etienne Harmonie avoided, when he could, the skirmishes between his country and England. He trusted neither, not since he had learned from his father, Georges, of the murder of his uncle Flourinot and little cousin Phillippe and of the fates of his aunt and Gennie. Gennie. . . . He sighed, thinking of her behind convent walls for the rest of her life. Huguenot women were not meant to be caged. They cherished their independent ways with a ferocity that matched the men's.

What unholy sloth, what rapacity, for a king to allow such a thing to happen to freeborn, loyal subjects. Etienne would never go back! Who was to say that he himself might not be murdered, as related by blood to a family in disgrace for the sin of not being Catholic?

The sun warmed his muscular back, tanned more darkly than his Indian companions'. Arms dangling over drawn-up knees, Etienne waited for them to complete their grisly business. He had been ordered to act as part of this raid. The governor of Trois-Rivières had threatened to revoke his trapper's license and those of any other coureurs who refused to "volunteer."

These Englishmen. What fools. Regimental soldiers wearing coats of bright red. Begging to be noticed! Their own faults to be killed. But the others. The ones in common dress ... Amazing how many English stayed permanently in the colonies. New France, he had realized in the years he had been here, had a problem persuading anyone to colonize. Soldiers took their tours and returned to France with full pockets. Rare was the man who brought a family to the wilderness!

Etienne had frequented English towns before war erupted. Dull, righteous clods, many of the inhabitants. They came to farm and rear families. The French came, like him, seeking adventure and fortunes in furs, or like the Black Robes, to claim this continent for Catholicism. Few came merely to live, to plant the soil or raise cattle. The English must lack a certain *joie de vivre*, he concluded. Their imaginations ran no further than gaudy coats where they were least appropriate.

The chief had paused to take another scalp and tuck it in his belt. His leggings were wet with dew and blood as he reached the edge of the meadow and smiled up at Etienne. A long bone pierced his nasal septum and rested against either cheek. Crescent-shaped bones hung like inverted horseshoes from his earlobes. Under the green coat, he wore four or five shirts, having lately decided to abandon nakedness in favor of dressing like the whiteskins. The coat appeared nearly new, and Etienne saw that it was quite bloody and rent with slashes.

"I have a gift for you." Chief Abinakis spoke in Mohican, a dialect of the Algonquins.

Etienne sprang down lightly from his perch on the log, to stand beside Abinakis. He knew the gift would be either some token of great honor, which he doubted since he had done as little as possible, or something the chief found useless and therefore was turning into something of use by giving it as a gift, which required of the recipient a gift in return.

Abinakis' hand reached inside the coat. He was missing a finger. He had dreamed one night, so Etienne had been told, that he had lost his finger and, promptly upon arising next morning, had cut if off, to appease whichever spirit he had offended.

What the chief pulled from an inner pocket of the green coat was not a trinket but a letter. "Important papers your chiefs will pay much for," he announced solemnly.

Etienne took the envelope. It was addressed in a blocky scrawl to a Mr. William Roebuck, Germantown Post Road, Pennsylvania. He opened the envelope and scanned the unfinished letter. He had never learned to read more than a few words of English, although he could speak it fairly well. *Boston, June 1745. Honour'd Sir & Madame:* . . . He read quickly what followed. The chief watched in greedy concentration.

"It is a family letter," he said in the chief's dialect. "The dead soldier speaks of his little brothers and of his wedding day. . . . Not a war letter, Chief Abinakis. My chiefs would pay nothing for this."

Abinakis looked disappointed, unwilling to take it back and forego his gift.

Etienne understood. He smiled. "But I would be pleased to receive this letter as a gift for myself, if you will allow me to give you something in return."

Abinakis smiled. "Since that is your desire, I will allow it."

Abinakis was a good man in his own way. He observed strict codes of honor himself and expected the same of his men. At the moment, among his other decorations, he was wearing a crucifix.

"Are you a Christian, Chief Abinakis?" Etienne said suddenly.

Abinakis chose not to hear.

"Christ was a Frenchman, you know. Crucified by the English."

Abinakis turned slowly to him. "So the Black Robes say. But I ask them: 'Do Iroquois warriors go to Christ's heaven?' And they say, 'Yes, my son, all who believe journey to be with Christ after they go to sleep.' " Abinakis drew himself up. "Abinakis does not sleep with the Iroquois!"

Etienne hid a smile. All the Algonquin tribes hated and feared the Iroquois. He knew the priests would never convert them. He thought of his uncle Flourinot and his family. The priests could not convert them either. Suddenly he made a decision.

"Chief Abinakis, I would like to have the coat, too."

The chief scowled. It was a fine coat. His squaws could cleanse the blood and mend the tears.

"I will give you a new coat, one that has belonged to no one but Abinakis, great chief of the Mohicans." He would send the coat and the letter to William Roebuck. Etienne could not have said why he was doing this, only that somehow it eased his own pain a little.

Abinakis made up his mind. He slipped off the coat and presented it disinterestedly to Etienne.

Etienne folded the coat over his arm. He would of course not mention the manner in which the son had met his death.

 t's the *Superbe*—looks to be sixty guns, sir!" reported the mate on the *Massachusetts*, peering through his spyglass. "And the *Mermaid* and the *Launceston*, forty guns each those are, if memory serves. Praise the Lord, sir!"

"Aye, indeed," said Captain Sparhawk, at his side. "How d'ye like that, General Pepperrell?"

"You're a good man, Nathaniel Sparhawk," said Pepperrell with heartfelt relief.

As if by divine timing, the three magnificent British ships had topped the southern horizon just hours after the colonial fleet reached Canseau. Evidently Commodore Peter Warren had not waited for royal blessing. He had sailed immediately to aid the colonists.

The colonials had kept out of range of the French fleet bottling in Canseau. But the French were not idle. They, too, had spotted the relief ships. Pepperrell asked for the glass and watched the frantic activity aboard all French vessels as they prepared to sail.

"This may be the easiest victory of the war, gentlemen. Our opposition is leaving." He swung the glass between ships and shore for several minutes, then turned to Sparhawk. "Let's get a few of our men ashore. I've an idea the French are not waiting for stragglers."

Within minutes of the French fleet's retreat, a rowboat was lowered from the *Massachusetts*, with Thomas Roebuck, Peter Sparhawk, and three riflemen sitting between the oarsmen. Their instructions were to seek out a French soldier with familiarity of conditions at Fort Louisbourg and bring him to Pepperrell.

Shortly after the boat was launched, a similar craft left the *Superbe* and came along side the *Massachusetts*.

"Permission to come aboard, sir!" called a clipped British voice.

Permission granted, the Jacob's ladder was lowered, and a young naval officer swung on deck. Ignoring the mate's salute, he said to the assembled men, "Take me to William Pepperrell."

The men suffered a moment of shocked embarrassment for their leader at this crude breach of etiquette. Wolcott spoke. "Young man, are you seeking General William Pepperrell, our commander-in-chief?"

"I—yes. Sir. I have a message from Admiral Warren, commander-in-chief . . ."

No one moved.

"Of—of his Majesty's Colonial Navy."

"*Admiral* Warren? I'll be bound he's never set foot in an American colony! Commander-in-chief indeed!" sputtered Captain Sparhawk.

Pepperrell appeared on deck. "I am General Pepperrell, son."

"Admiral Warren's papers, sir. His commission from the duke of Marlborough. Sir." He snapped a packet of documents at Pepperrell.

Sparhawk made a move toward the insolent officer, but Wolcott seized his arm.

"Admiral Warren also instructs me to invite you aboard the *Superbe* to participate in tactical discussions. Sir."

"Instruct him to meet us here for tactical discussions," Sparhawk burst out.

Pepperrell lifted his eyebrows as if to say, Are we returning like for like? He turned to the British officer. "Please extend to Commodore Warren our profound gratitude for his timely appearance. Inform him that we will shortly have aboard a French prisoner for purposes of interrogation, and his presence is invited."

———◆———

Stepping ashore at Canseau, Roebuck and Sparhawk found that their task had been made easy. As the hardy fisherfolk realized they were delivered, they rounded up the abandoned French militia and imprisoned them in the largest house in the village. Proudly they ushered their rescuers to the prisoners.

Most were in the blue-and-white uniform of the French navy. "Any of you speak English?" asked Thomas.

Several of the men responded. Thomas let them talk a few minutes. It was apparent they felt betrayed, being left behind. All were crewmen, save two from the garrison at Fort Louisbourg. He and Peter questioned these two closely, then chose the man whose eagerness did not seem to overshadow his honesty.

Returning to the flagship, where Pepperrell waited, Thomas studied their prisoner frankly. His cheeks were hollow and his skin grayish. It was the closest he had ever been to "the enemy." The enemy looked exactly like one of themselves: bundled in tricorn jammed over a scarf wound over neck and ears and thrust into a greatcoat, mittens, leggings over wool trousers, and well-worn boots. Spring had not yet come to this lonely, windswept pile of rocks.

"Where are you from originally?" Thomas asked.

The soldier seemed not at all intimidated at the separation from his brothers-in-arms. "Marseilles, sir."

"Did you know any families from Le Havre?" he asked impulsively.

"Quite a distance from Marseilles, sir."

"Harmonie. Flourinot Harmonie."

"No, sir. Friend of yours?"

Thomas smiled. "His daughter is to be my wife. I have a letter from her," he admitted self-consciously. "This one is in French. I confess I have yet to read it."

"Maybe Frenchy will do the honors," teased Peter.

The Frenchman grinned. "You have the letter with you?"

"Always," Peter murmured.

Thomas ripped off a mitten and stood up to dig the letter from his pocket. It had arrived the day they left Boston. The men had been warned to expect no more mail deliveries in either direction for several weeks, possibly longer. The rowboat tilted precariously in the choppy waters, until Thomas sat down again.

Reverently he unfolded the letter and passed it to his prisoner, who mouthed the words and then smiled.

"It is a love letter, m'sieu."

Thomas glanced at Peter, who had the grace to discover a sudden interest elsewhere.

" 'For the first time I do not feel so badly knowing that Papa may be dead, because I know that you are right—*le bon Dieu* has sent you to me. As I write this, I see your dear face shining before me, so strong and full of love. Oh, Thomas, I cannot wait to be your wife, to live together on our own farm. Will Ohio be like Le Havre? I wonder. Much more, dear one, I long for, but modesty forbids my writing it in a letter. *Pardonnez moi* for forcing you to seek translation, but I could not bear M. Z. knowing my innermost feelings. It will be different with a stranger. Come home soon, my own dear love. Gennie.' "

The Frenchman's eyes lingered longingly over the letter before he surrendered it.

Peter whistled silently. "I wish a lady loved me like that."

The prisoner said, "I have a wife, and a babe by this time, God willing, back in Marseilles. My time is almost up. D'you think the English will let me go home?"

"I will do what I can." Thomas tucked the letter securely away just as the boat bumped the side of the *Massachusetts*.

For the first time the Frenchman looked uneasy. "You seem a decent, Christian fellow. What are they really going to do with me?"

"Just ask questions. Be truthful, and you have nothing to fear."

Minutes later they were standing in the wardroom, thawing their chilled limbs before a tidy fire in the grate, awaiting the arrival of Warren. Thomas wondered at the lack of eagerness among the officers as they waited for their benefactor. Even Peter's father cut off questions with a surly shake of the head. The usual amiability of the American officers was further cooled as Peter Warren swept into the room, preceded and announced by a young naval officer with a decidedly arrogant manner.

Hostility as thick as smoke simmered through the introductions. But even the most resentful of the colonial leaders had to admit that Peter Warren—admiral or commodore—cut a fine figure: tall, lean, and tanned of face, wearing a perfectly cut blue coat with crisp lace cuffs and starched cravat, and fine trousers that revealed supple, muscular legs.

The prisoner, with the promise of a hearty English meal after the interrogation, was eager to talk. The garrison at Fort Louisbourg was mutinous, he told them. Provisions were rationed. The few families who inhabited Cape Breton, along with a straggling of Indians, blamed the militia for commandeering all the stores of grain and meat for their own use.

There was also a poor convent on the island, whose nuns did their best to care for the sickly and feed the starving. Not that anyone outside the church knew how much food they actually had—even the king's men had no authority to search holy grounds.

"Are we to believe, then, that unless the provision ships come quickly from France, your population is in actual danger of starving?" asked Warren.

"That is not putting it too strongly, sir."

"And the ships are expected—"

"They are on the way now. . . ." Several officers exchanged glances. "They always time their arrival about the time the ice breaks up. And none too soon this year; it's been a bad one."

Pepperrell looked around. "Gentlemen? Any more questions? Yes, Roebuck?"

"Sir, I suggest we ask the prisoner to draw us a map, as near as he can recall, of the layout inside the fort, including placement of artillery batteries. If he's of a mind, a layout of the town itself would not be amiss." Seeing doubt on several faces—none of them would do such a thing!—he added quickly, "In exchange we would give the prisoner our word to drop him unharmed at the port of his choice after the battle is won."

The prisoner flashed him a look of gratitude that was not lost on Roger Wolcott. Wolcott came immediately to his aid. "That is a splendid idea, Roebuck." He looked expectantly at Pepperrell, pointedly ignoring Warren.

"Possibilities," agreed Pepperrell. "Have the prisoner held 'tween decks while we discuss it."

"And feed him?" added Thomas.

"And feed him," agreed Pepperrell, with a grin.

Thomas ushered the man to the custody of two of his men, with instructions, and returned to the wardroom.

". . . French warships. We have no vessels to equal that tonnage," Warren was saying. "We have not the cannon to equal her. We'll blockade Louisbourg and use our infantry after the blockade has broken their will."

Pepperrell shook his head. "France has spent twenty-five years fortifying Louisbourg. Despite the prisoner's words, starving them out could take a year. Unless we use the troops for assault, help from France will arrive before Louisbourg capitulates."

"I will deploy the infantry as I deem wise," said Warren.

Thoughtfully, William Pepperrell studied the man who had been so eagerly awaited as ally, but who now seemed more like adversary. "Good," he said. "And I will tell you how you may use your ships."

Several men laughed, realizing the ridiculousness of the statement. It broke the tension slightly. Peter Warren saw nothing humorous at all.

"Look here, my dear Pepperrell—"

"Commodore . . . Admiral Warren," Pepperrell said mildly, "I was born in the colonies. I am as familiar with these shores, the weather, the moods of my men, as you are with your homes in England and Antigua. It is not in His Majesty's best interests to put you in charge of my men, nor I of yours. We shall coordinate our efforts; my men must be transported on your ships, but I and my staff shall devise the strategy on land, both its timing and the manner. Together, with Providence at hand, we shall drive the Papists of Louisbourg out and the French navy back to France."

Nods and mutters of approval greeted these conciliating words. Warren quickly took the measure of his associates. Inwardly he fumed at the arrogance of these rough colonials. Not a military mind among them. Oh, in England how quickly they would be humbled!

Warren inclined his handsome head gracefully. "As you say, together we shall win the day."

·C·H·A·P·T·E·R· 19 ·

enri Zellaire walked into his house. He had been unusually quiet the past few days, avoiding even Marie Therese, whose company he usually sought. But now, finding her alone, he said, "Marie Therese, there are matters I must discuss with you."

A month had passed since a brokenhearted William Roebuck had ridden into Germantown and informed them of Thomas's death in an Indian raid somewhere in Massachusetts. Henri had not been idle since then. Now he sat at the table and covered Marie Therese's hand with his own, freckled and sunburned. She glanced at him in surprise, but did not remove her hand. His blue eyes reflected an unguarded tenderness. *"Ma chérie,* since you came, our home has been a different place. You know I care for you in a way I have not felt about anyone since my wife died."

"Henri, please."

"Wait. Hear me. I have not pressed you because I knew that you held out hope that your husband was alive." His glance shifted to a folded paper carried in his free hand. "It was Providence that caused a member of your own family to discover Thomas's coat."

"The ways of God are strange," mused Marie Therese. "He took away Gennie's Thomas, but restored to us her cousin."

"Living no farther away than Trois-Rivières, less than two weeks' journey for an experienced rider. I sent a messenger to Etienne Harmonie. I know this is painful for you, my dear, but it is best to know."

Marie Therese looked startled. "To know what?"

"That your husband and your son are indeed dead," said Henri. He unfolded the letter. "Here it is. Read it at your leisure. Etienne says that his father, your late husband's brother, was permitted to remove the bodies and give them a Christian burial by night. Georges Flourinot was forbidden to communicate with you at the time. Etienne promises to visit you after the war," he added.

If Henri had feared an outburst from her, he was relieved that she merely looked away and then gazed stonily at him, her eyes dry. "I have known. I have felt it. Thank you, Henri. I will read the letter. Gennie must be told."

He nodded. A comforting smile creased his face. He took up her hand again. "Then, dear lady, I am free at last to ask you: Will you be my wife?"

Marie Therese bowed her head. "Yes."

He squeezed her hand. "Now," he said briskly, after what he considered a decent interval. "About Gennie. Goodman Amos has asked again to marry her. I put him off once, you remember. With Thomas gone, it would be good for her to marry. Then, when children come along, she'll forget all the unhappiness of the last year. She'll be a wonderful little mother. Just to watch her with my children—"

"But, Henri! Gennie does not love Mr. Amos. Why, she cared as much for Thomas as if they had been officially betrothed!"

"Nonsense. Girlish nonsense. And you, my girl, are too romantic!" Zellaire tried to sound playful. "Since when do sixteen-year-olds know their own minds?"

Marie Therese stared at him, her dark eyes trying to penetrate his reasoning. "She is seventeen."

Zellaire's mouth turned down into a hard line. "My mind is made up. I would have honored my word to young Roebuck. Now that he is dead, I see no reason to postpone a marriage arrangement for her. Goodman Amos has offered to marry her. He is an upright, pious man. Though he might be considered to be a trifle old for her—," Zellaire had the grace to look away, "he has ample means to support a wife. Which young Roebuck did not," he added defensively. "You may help me secure Gennie's acceptance of this circumstance, or you may hinder. Either way, I have made up my mind."

"Henri, you cannot possibly expect me to want my own daughter to marry a man she does not love! Why would you ask such a thing? Surely you will give her time—"

"No."

Marie Therese pulled her hand away and stood up. She threw back her head and sent a piercing glance at the man she had agreed to marry. "Gennie and I will work for you; we will fulfill our contracts. Or you may sell us. I understand from Gennie that is your right. But to do as you ask is unchristian!"

Zellaire's face suffused in a bright flush of anger, until his freckles all seemed to run together. "Very well, madame. You seem to forget who you are here. I shall speak to your daughter myself."

Marie Therese swallowed her fright. She said in a cold voice, "Have I your permission to go upstairs?"

Zellaire waved her away. With frustration he watched her straight back receding. It was not going at all well! He had thought she would be pleased. It was a great coup for Gennie, a young woman without a dowry securing such a rich husband.

Zellaire saw the two fine workmen promised him by Amos slipping from his grasp. When would he ever have enough money himself to afford such help? And good, sound slaves at that! A lifetime investment! He thought of himself talked about in the tavern. That Henri Zellaire is a shrewd one! To parlay one serving wench into two strong workers and ally himself with a rich family to boot!

He hardened his heart against the image of Marie Therese's frightened face. Women! She would get over it. For a minute there he had actually been tempted to do as this indentured servant asked. Well, he would *still* have her. And his workmen.

Noiselessly Marie Therese opened the door of the bedroom, erasing the agitation from her face. She had never been a very beautiful woman. Even when young, the somewhat strong planes of her face had suggested determination rather than prettiness.

Gennie was propped cross-legged on her bed, writing in her book. Her lips were parted slightly, the corner of her full lower lip caught between her teeth as she wrote. Suffering had deepened the hollows beneath her eyes, emphasizing a beauty that was both sensuous and vulnerable. *Just the sort*, Marie Therese thought sadly, *to tempt a man like Goodman Amos.*

She was wearing a homespun dress with flared skirt and blue sash. The bodice gaped open, as though she had been in the act of dressing when seized with the impulse to write. She lifted one finger to scratch at the hollow of her throat, then trailed it absently down between the creamy, ripe swell of her breasts.

Marie Therese was unaware that she was shaking her head. No. She would never do as Henri asked. Never would she cause her daughter any more pain than she had already endured. She was heartened to see that Gennie did look a little brighter than she had since the letter reporting Thomas's death.

Suddenly Gennie looked up. She smiled warmly. "I was just writing in my commonplace book. Sister Margarethe said I must write every day to keep a flowing hand."

Marie Therese smiled. "What are you writing?"

Gennie hesitated. She closed the book. "I will tell you only if you do not try to dissuade me."

A puzzled frown crossed her mother's face. She closed the door and came to perch on the end of Gennie's bed.

"Thomas is not dead, Mama."

Marie Therese looked startled. "He lives in Christ . . ."

Firmly Gennie shook her head. Her eyes glowed tenderly. "I have prayed about it every day. And every day I have become more strongly convinced that he is not dead. What do we know? Only that his coat was found and a letter. Mr. Roebuck has had no word from Thomas's regiment either, he said so himself."

"Gennie, you saw his coat—"

"No! He is not dead, I tell you!" She clasped her book to her bosom. Her back stiffened. Her mouth set in a firm line. "Thomas told me that God meant for him to care for me. I believe him. And I just will not listen to any more talk about his death." Her eyes flashed, daring her mother to contradict her. Suddenly she smiled sweetly. "Mama, would you like to see what I have been working on?"

Marie Therese was so stunned she was speechless.

Almost shyly, Gennie slid off the bed and lifted the lid of a large saddleback trunk with bronze fittings. She withdrew a long, white cravat, its edges rolled and sewn with barely visible stitches. Into one end she had embroidered the initials T R, in a romantic, embellished script. "I made it from the linen pieces left after we did the boys' shirts. It is for Thomas to wear on our wedding day."

Marie Therese's eyes blurred with tears. She had difficulty seeing the stitches as she bent her head to examine the workmanship. "It is beautiful, Gennie. Your best work. "*Ah, Lord!* she prayed. *Is this, in your mercy, a step to healing her sorrow?*

Suddenly they heard Zellaire's voice. He was summoning Gennie. Hastily Gennie buttoned her bodice and smoothed her skirts. She smiled at her mother. Marie Therese's throat constricted as she followed Gennie to the head of the stairs.

Zellaire was sitting near the foot of the stairs. "Gennie! Good. Come down, please. I wish to speak to you."

"Yes, m'sieu?"

ape Breton Island was shaped like a fat, crevassed U. The fortress rose on the northeast tip, awesome and forbidding, from a boulder-strewn shore, against which waves crashed with unrelenting fury. Fort Louisbourg's landward sides were heavily fortified. Artillery batteries ringed it stategically from rocky promontories that gave out over the forested island and stood on ramparts that abutted the walls of the town. The town itself huddled in the shadow of the fortress, much as villages in ancient and medieval times lived under the protection of castles.

Winds rolled the tips of the trees in blue-black undulations, revealing here and there the penetrating blue of the deep, cratered bay that gutted the center of the island. Across the northern points of the island ran Cabot Strait, now impassable. Once the ice broke up, ships could sail the strait, into the Gulf of Saint Lawrence, and from there into the Saint Lawrence River and southwest 500 miles to Quebec.

Warren had no difficulty distributing his ships for a total seaward siege. Pepperrell used the time to have Warren's artillery officers coach his men in the loading and handling of cannon. It amused the naval officers to think these recruits expected to handle cannon well in days, when they needed months or years.

Cannonading by the ships forced the French to abandon their seaward batteries, while 4,000 troops plunged through surf and across rocks to go to ground in the forests.

The commanders mustered the men on the hills, in plain sight of town, that first day, where they audaciously serenaded the French with tavern songs. Then they threw themselves into transporting supplies and ordinance.

No roads crossed the island. Cannon were off-loaded onto flat-keeled fishing boats and run ashore between rocks. Some of the cannon balls were too large for English cannon; headquarters had ordered them made in French calibre, confident that as enemy batteries were captured, usable cannon would be found.

They felled trees, built roads, and filled ditches. Lacking oxen, the men hauled cannon mile after mile, by ropes over their shoulders. Sweating, straining, abetted by the promise of daily rum rations, the enthusiastic men believed themselves invincible. Their cause was God's; success was inevitable.

Parson Moody strode among the infantry companies and artillery batteries, shouting encouragement, ignoring the bawdy songs that lightened their prodigious labors, reprimanding them only for cursing. "If we do not win, it will be God's judgment on your profanity!"

At last the cannon were in place behind crude breastworks. On sea and land the siege was complete. Thomas and his men were deployed behind barriers erected of hogsheads filled with earth, just beyond artillery range of the French battery above them. Here they waited.

A month passed. Occasionally cannonballs soared toward them, to flop ingloriously in the mud. When boredom overcame them, men would dash out, under fire, to retrieve and fire them back. The French tried the same tactic, only to discover to their dismay that some of the New Englanders' rifles could pick them off while still two hundred yards away.

Wait. Nothing to do but wait. It had rained and sleeted for the past three days. Spring had come to Pennsylvania weeks ago, mused Thomas, sitting with his back against a rock, dreaming of Gennie. He basked in the warmth of his conjured images. She was picking wild flowers. In his mittened hand he held her letter. Between the lines of French, he had printed the English. But he savored the French phrases on his tongue. Truly, French was the language of love. She loved him. She wanted him. He thought of how it would be on their wedding night. Oh, Gennie, Gennie!

Thomas shivered. His eyes snapped open, clear and ice blue with the reality of their situation. Could they starve out the French before ships-of-war arrived from the mother country to pound them out of the water? The ice was beginning to break up in the Strait. If Warren's fleet was defeated, men on the island would be at the mercy of the French.

Within the besieged town, Thomas knew, French families, soldiers, priests, and a scattering of Indians also waited. Nothing very glorious about this war, so far. He kindled a small fire, propped his wet boots as close as was safe, closed his eyes again, and returned to thoughts of Gennie.

A young officer stood on the rampart of the French battery, watching the English below. He smiled to see someone appear out of the shadow of a rock to build a small fire. Foolish, to think that by sitting there they could have any effect on the French position. If they only knew what was in store for them. The English would soon get a taste of war not to their liking.

"André," said a soft voice.

He whirled. "Anne! Darling!"

Anne Duchambon, daughter of the commandant of Louisbourg, stood smiling before him, her heavy cape ruffled by the wind, the top pushed back to show her honey-gold curls. She was swinging a picnic basket.

"Darling, you should not be here. It isn't safe!"

"I was lonesome," she pouted. "There is nothing to do in town. I thought it a lovely day for a picnic."

"In the *rain?*"

Her green eyes flirted outrageously at him. "All sorts of marvelous things happen in the rain. Besides, it has stopped."

The men in the battery were grinning and nudging each other. Some had sweethearts or wives in town, too.

"If he is not hungry, I'll picnic with you, Mademoiselle Duchambon!" The gallant offer was seconded half a dozen times. Anne blushed with pleasure. "There was little to create a picnic with, but I did find some of Papa's brandy . . ."

André was laughing now as his clever sweetheart passed the brandy to his comrades, who then discreetly withdrew. He led her to a sheltered corner of the battery and pulled off his heavy coat for her to sit upon.

"You are adorable," he murmured as they settled in the corner. "Did you really find something to put in that basket?"

"Of course!" She pulled out two biscuits. "Plovers' eggs, pickled in champagne and nutmeg." Nuts, dried apricots, and apples appeared next: "A compote of brandied fruit." Last she opened a small packet of beef preserved in sour cherries and bear fat and pronounced it roast grouse stuffed with chestnuts and oysters.

André barely looked at the pitiful repast. He grinned at Anne. "What an enchantress you are. I hope all our children take after you—we'll never go hungry!"

Anne lowered her lashes. "Thank you, my lord."

André pulled her gently to him, cradling her in his lap. He kissed her gently. So good . . . so good. He did not want to ever let her go. The hunger, the longing, the separation. This cat-and-mouse war . . . Suddenly he realized she was struggling in his arms. He released her. "I am sorry, darling . . ."

She nodded, then clung fiercely to him, her face against his chest. "Oh, André, sometimes I am so frightened. What are they waiting for?"

He did not know the answer. The longer the English waited, the greater chance the French fleet would catch them. "It is in the hands of God. Anne, you must go back now." He sprang to his feet and helped her up. "Thank you for the food."

"Wait!" From the bottom of her basket she withdrew a bottle of champagne and two glasses. "First a toast."

"What . . . ?"

"It's our anniversary, silly. We have been betrothed three months. Surely you have not forgotten!"

André laughed. "How could I?" He uncorked the bottle and poured them each a glass. They stood facing each other on the rampart, not caring that Englishmen below had lined up to wave and shriek for attention, nor that their own men were casting eyes naked with envy. Against a roiling yellow sky, angry with clouds, they lifted their glasses.

"*A ta santé,*" she whispered.

"*A ta santé.*"

From below, Thomas watched as they embraced one last time and she turned away. The Frenchman turned. He seemed to be looking directly at Thomas.

" 'Allo, *Anglais!*" He lifted the bottle. "*A votre santé!*" With a flourish, he drank.

"How do you like the bold beggar?" laughed Thomas. "Drinking to our health yet!"

ennie Harmonie! Where you been keepin' yourself? Res' the family in town?"

"Rosalind! How nice to see you!" Rosalind Hambleton was wearing a well-made homespun linen dyed a sober indigo, with a fluffy shawl of bright blue wool plaid looped in a triangle over her dress. Her hair was pulled back into a double-coiled bun. She looked eminently dignified. But the sparkling eyes and full red lips hinted at inner gaiety.

Gennie could not help thinking how—how *glowy* she appeared and told her so.

Rosalind pealed with laughter. "It's 'caise I am now a free woman!"

"You *are*? But how?"

"I bought my freedom, girl! Mr. Hambleton done set a price, an' I been workin' ever since, puttin' some by every time I delivered a baby."

"You are a midwife. I had forgotten."

"Honey, I birthed half the chilrun in this town, under the age of ten!"

"Where are you living?"

"Same place, on Mr. Hambleton's property. On'y now I pay rent!" she declared proudly.

Impulsively Gennie embraced her. "I am so happy for you. God bless you, Rosalind!"

"So how is it with you? Your English done improved mightily."

Gennie was tempted to confide. How desperately she needed a friend! Instead she said, "No better than you warned me."

Immediately Rosalind's face changed. "Anything I can do?"

Gennie smiled and shook her head.

"If they is, you know where to find me."

Gennie bid her friend good-bye and hurried down the street toward the schoolhouse, which was next to the French Reformed Church in the next block. Henri Zellaire had business in Philadelphia today, and Gennie had seized the opportunity to walk into Germantown and try to seek a way out of her predicament.

How could M. Zellaire be so nice on one hand and so stubborn on the other?

Deep inside, she must have known that Papa and Phillippe were dead, for when her mother had broken the news, she found that her grief was partly relief at knowing the truth at last. Still, how could Mama even have thought of marrying Henri Zellaire after Papa! No one would ever measure up to Papa.

She hoped that Parson Cullers could help her. She walked past the church and the tiny house where he lived, to wait in the shade of a hickory tree outside the closed doors of the frame schoolhouse. During the week, Parson Cullers was also schoolmaster. She hoped her wait would not be too long. The walk home would take an hour, and she wanted to arrive before M. Zellaire.

The doors opened, and a bevy of shouting boys burst through.

"Gennie, hi!" said Jean Zellaire. "You come to meet us?"

"No, honey, you children start on home. I will be there in a little while."

The girls swarmed out after the boys, equally rambunctious, though hampered by skirts from achieving the tremendous leaps from top step to street accomplished by the boys.

"Parson Cullers?" Gennie peeped inside the door after the children had left.

"Miss Harmonie, what a pleasant surprise. I always enjoy seeing your smiling face when I look down from the pulpit Sundays." Cullers was a thin, reedy man with a stiff posture, but possessing a beautiful baritone voice, which was always a surprise to its hearers. Gennie had heard it said that it was in compensation for having been ignored in the Lord's body-building department.

He pulled two benches away from the desks and positioned them opposite each other. He motioned her to one, sat on the other, and placed his hands on his kneecaps with a small but firm slap. "Now, Miss Harmonie," he said briskly. "How may I help you?"

Gennie perched erectly on the bench facing the parson. She smoothed her white gloves over the backs of her hands and then with her fingers plaited the folds of her skirt into symmetrical pleats, as if achieving a material order would still the turmoil inside. She was already beginning to regret that she had come. How could she expect him to care about her problems? But he cared about the children he taught. That much was obvious.

She looked up and smiled hesitantly. "The children all seem so happy. You must be a fine teacher."

He smiled. "Did you like school in France?"

"Oh, yes!" Gennie lifted her mother's berry-colored wool shawl carefully away from her hair and settled it about her shoulders. Her hair was braided in one long, thick plait that hung down her back. Little tendrils curled about her ears.

Most charming, Parson Cullers was thinking. The color of the shawl brought a nip of berry pink to her cheeks and showed off the chestnut richness of her hair.

He recalled how tiny and pinched she had seemed the first time he had seen her, when Henri Zellaire had brought her and her mother to church one Sunday and asked the congregation to join him in thanks for their safe arrival. She had filled out. She was becoming a beautiful young woman, he realized, thinking suddenly it was time he himself had a wife.

"You are looking very well, Miss Harmonie. How do you like Germantown after—what is it?—nearly a year?"

"Very well, sir. Parson Cullers, may I speak in confidence? I need your help."

"Certainly," he said, not above feeling flattered. Something about her brought out the protective instinct in him. He was nearly thirty. Yes, time he did think of settling down. "May I offer you a glass of water? I'm afraid it's all—"

"No, thank you," she said, smiling.

What a lovely smile, he thought, a caring, tender smile. No wonder the Zellaire children doted on Gennie. "Do you need tutoring, then?" thinking that perhaps her obvious discomfiture was caused by an inability to master English.

"Oh, no, sir," she laughed, hiding her embarrassment. "The children are very good teachers. I help them with sums, and they help me with English. It is Monsieur Zellaire I have come about."

"Oh?"

"You see, sir, we must work for him for six years yet, my mother and me, to repay him for our passage to America."

"*I,* not me," he corrected her absently. "And you do not like the arrangement?"

"It isn't that, Parson Cullers, I *want* to stay with Monsieur Zellaire and work for him and the children and be with my mother." Gennie bit her lip. The parson was leaning forward, not at all frightening, his eyes reassuring.

"A certain gentleman has told Monsieur Zellaire that he wishes to marry me. Monsieur Zellaire is—"

The parson leaned back. ". . . Willing and you are not."

"Yes, sir . . . I am already betrothed!" Gennie burst out. "Monsieur Zellaire said that as soon as Mr. Thomas Roebuck came back from the war, we could be married."

"Ah, yes, Thomas Roebuck. He did not attend my church, of course, but I know his family. A tragic thing. The first lad from Germantown."

Tears brimmed and clung to Gennie's thick lashes. "He is not dead." Her voice dropped to an intense pitch. "I know he is not dead! And now Monsieur Zellaire plans to ask you to read the banns this Sunday. And Goodman Amos is older than my own father was! And I don't think he ever bathes!" The back of her gloved fingers flew to her lips. "I am sorry, Parson Cullers. That was unkind. But do you see? What can I do? I have come to you, sir! My sweet Savior does not want me to marry that man!"

"How can any of us know what God wants for us?" the parson mused, half to himself.

Gennie looked at him in consternation. "You mean you do not know? When you are doing what God wants, don't you feel just filled up with wonderful feelings? It was that way, back in France, when our family worshiped Him together. And it was that way when Thomas Roebuck told me God wanted him to take care of me. I know he isn't dead, sir, I know it! They found his coat, that is all. Please help me!"

Cullers' lips drew into a strict line, as if confronted by a distasteful duty. "Gennie, management of the affairs of young ladies your age is properly left to those older and wiser. They know what is best for you. If you were an orphan of fourteen or under, the town council could forbid your marriage."

"But why isn't Mama's word enough? She knows how I feel!" Tears coursed unchecked down her cheeks as she appealed to him. She had never felt so powerless.

"Your mother is also indentured. While you are in Monsieur Zellaire's employ, he has the right to make these decisions for you." But even while he told her this, Cullers was outraged. Heartless. It was utterly heartless. Zellaire was ever one to take advantage of a situation. Parson Cullers could not help wondering what the man stood to gain by such blatant abuse of his legal rights. Perhaps he should look into the matter himself. He rose.

"I will see what I can do, Gennie." He gazed with compassion at her lowered head, at the gloved fist resting against her forehead clutching the bit of embroidered handkerchief. "But I think you must be prepared. The law is on the side of Monsieur Zellaire."

"He does not own my soul!" she hissed, not moving.

"So I intend to remind him," he murmured. "So I intend. Shall we pray?"

Parson Cullers had been engaged on a yearly basis to teach and preach to the French-speaking population of Germantown, the town fathers being of the opinion that giving a parson tenure was tantamount to surrendering control of their church to England. Many other villages and towns in the colonies followed the same practice. But however modest the parson's station, an invitation to call upon him was rarely ignored. No one knew when his immortal soul might be in peril, nor what damage its owner might do by neglecting a call from his spiritual leader.

Henri Zellaire's visit to the modest home allotted for use by the parson lasted a scant twenty minutes. He left fuming with rage at Gennie, for exposing him to the humiliation of having to reveal his private affairs to that young whippersnapper. And as for Cullers! Wait until his contract came up for renewal!

He walked quickly through the town, head first, hat clamped tightly on, hands balled into fists. Then his step slowed. The way to win was to not let his anger rule his head. That was his cardinal rule, and it had made him a successful man. Marie Therese could be made to force her daughter's obedience. Ah. But he had a better idea.

"Gennie, I think of you as a daughter," he said to her, hours later, having sauntered into the barn as she finished the milking. "It grieves me that you do not return my affection."

"But I do, sir." Gennie patted the cow's flank and picked up her milk stool. Damp tendrils of hair were matted on her forehead where she had leaned against the cow.

"But not enough to come to me with your concerns. Why, if I had known how you felt about Mr. Amos, I would never have allowed for a moment—"

"Is it true, Monsieur Zellaire? Oh, I am so happy!" Gennie dropped the stool and flung her arms wide. Zellaire stepped backward in alarm.

"Now, wait. Let us consider."

Something in his tone told her to be wary. She immediately lost her air of relief and waited with held breath for his next words.

"The truth is, your mother and I—well, I love her. I have wanted to marry her for a long time. And I think she cares for me. Do you think she does, Gennie?"

"Yes, Monsieur Zellaire. She often says what a kind and good man you are." *But not good enough to marry,* Gennie thought.

Zellaire nodded, as if he could not agree more. "Did she also tell you that she will not marry me now?" Zellaire made an effort to look the tragic comedian. "No? No, of course she would not. She cares for you too much."

"Cares for me too much!"

"No, she won't marry me because she says to me, 'Henri, Gennie needs me. If Thomas were here, he would take care of my Gennie. But now there is no one. . . .' That is what she said to me, Gennie."

God would forgive him. After all, it was for the girl's own good, *n'est-ce pas?*

Fear spread its clammy fingers down into her stomach. "Mama will not marry you because there is no one to take care of me? Surely that is not the only reason, Monsieur Zellaire. I am a young woman. I do not need anyone. I can go on working for you—"

"Gennie, Gennie, how would it look, you a servant in the house where your mother is mistress? No, I suppose we must leave it in the hands of Providence." Zellaire sighed loudly and deeply. "Love is a strange and demanding thing, is it not, my dear? Well, thank you for listening to a disappointed man. Let us go in, the wind is turning chill. Here, let me help you carry the milk."

His words chilled her far more than any wind. Her mama, her beloved mama, who had sacrificed so much for her, was now prepared to deny her own love for her daughter's sake. In a depth of sadness such as she had not know since the days after Papa's and Phillippe's deaths, Gennie knew what she must do.

·C·H·A·P·T·E·R·22·

homas paced back and forth. Here two months and they had done nothing. During the worst of the cold, the high spirits of his men had not saved them from the effects of excessive exposure. Fever and diarrhea raged through the troops until at one time Thomas heard that barely half the infantry and artillery were fit for duty.

For the tenth time that morning he paused to study the French battery above them, a thousand yards up a broken, irregular slope. In his mind he saw details of the map drawn by their French prisoner from Canseau. "Why not?" he said with a sharp laugh. "Corporal!"

"Yes, sir?"

"Message to the next battery. Ask Lieutenant Sparhawk to meet me at ten at the halfway point." As the man left he went through his papers for his copy of the map. An hour later, leaving his sergeant in charge, he set out.

Thomas saw his friend approaching in the distance. At home in Boston, Sparhawk dressed the part of scion of a prominent whaling family, foppishly at times. His hair had been long and silky clean, his luxuriant moustache trimmed and combed to a fare-thee-well. Visiting the Sparhawks, Thomas had looked like a poor relation.

Gone now were fine clothes; for officers and men on the batteries, warmest dark woolens had replaced fine broadcloth. Boots roomy enough to accommodate inner layers of felt, rags, or even leaves replaced their polished counterparts.

Since the loss of his greatcoat, Thomas had reverted to his trapping clothes, easy and warm and comfortably bulky.

"Good morning. Looks like a bonny day," he said as Peter climbed to meet him.

Peter's moustache had suffered at the hands of a novice barber. It drooped into his untamed beard. He grinned, a flash of white teeth in a cave of hair. "Bonny for sitting around in the mud again?"

Thomas answered good-humoredly, "I judged you might be ready for a bit of action."

A musket shot pinged on a rock some distance away. Both turned toward the French battery, code named Green. Peter doffed his hat and bowed.

"Forgive me! *Bon jour* to you, too!" he shouted. "And we are planning to make it even more pleasant!" He turned with whetted interest back to Thomas.

"Our Frenchy's map shows forty-two pounders in the Green battery. Did you know that?"

"Of course. Which is why we are dug in here and not up there."

"And we do happen to have forty-two-pound balls in our ordinance on the beach."

"Righto. To use when we capture the French cannon."

"Or steal one."

Peter laughed. "You are a lunatic, Thomas."

"Getting tired of doing nothing. I've been studying it all morning. The Green isn't actually that far from shore. Our ships could sail in close enough to shell the Frenchies and chase them out for a while. Long enough for us to get up there and help ourselves."

Peter shook his head. "It's a mad scheme. That battery is placed so that even if it is overrun, the guns can't be turned against the fortress. The hill is too steep, and it's too close."

"But from here—"

"That's like selling the skin of a bear before you catch it."

A devil-may-care grin split Thomas's face. "We lift it from its carriage and tip it down the hill. Easy."

"Men with ropes could haul it down, I suppose, with cover fire . . . Let's put it in my battery."

Thomas shook his head. "We have a perfect angle to do some real damage to the fort. You send some men to the beach to bring up the balls while we are emplacing it.

"I'll talk to Wolcott. Pray that Pepperrell and Warren are not feuding today!"

"Aye," agreed Peter.

Major General Wolcott thought it a splendid idea, certain to demoralize the French, if successful.

General Pepperrell on the other hand knew that Admiral Warren would think the scheme harebrained, reckless, and unmilitary. With which estimate Pepperrell would agree. Therefore, while he gave Roebuck and Wolcott his blessing, he thought it wise to tell Warren only that they required a shelling of the Green battery.

The time was set for early next morning, when fogs concealed the American positions and when, if the sun did break through, it would be in the eyes of the defenders.

At first light, shelling began, the heavy boom of ships' cannon followed ticking-seconds later by dull thuds as the balls landed. They had some difficulty finding the range. When at last they did home in, the New Englanders poised below saw the Frenchmen manning the battery scatter like roaches in the light.

Peter Sparhawk directed his sharpshooters into position. As the last boom died away, Thomas and 300 men zigzagged up the hill. French fire scattered from a broad arc above their heads, answered from below.

Pepperrell, watching through his glass from aboard the *Massachusetts*, moved his lips in fervent prayer for the safety of his men. Warren, on the bridge of the *Superbe*, muttered, "No discipline! What in God's name did they spend their drill time on? Look at them! I've yet to see a single banner, a single man in formation!"

"True, sir," said his aide. "But what a show! Look! They've actually stormed the battery! Oh, good show!"

Warren swung down the glass and scowled at him. "Get ashore. Find Major General Wolcott. Ask him just what is going on!"

Thomas and his men poured over the ramparts of the Green battery, immediately ringing it and laying down rounds of deadly fire while the gunnery crew raced from one cannon to the next, exclaiming over the number and power of the weapons.

"Lieutenant Roebuck! Here! A forty-two pounder, just like you said!" The man uttered an exclamation of dismay.

Thomas ran over. "What, Higgins?"

"They spiked 'em, sir! They spiked the blasted touchholes!"

"Over here, sir, look! Bombshells, big ones, a hundred of them! And cartridges!"

"That's the lad!" shouted Thomas. "You, you, and you: Get relay teams together and start passing that stuff down the hill."

"What about the cannon, sir?"

"Any other damage?"

"No, sir."

"Then truss it up. We can drill out the touchhole back home." Using a pike as lever, they pried the cannon off its carriage mounts. Dozens of men on ropes maneuvered the heavy cannon to the top of the battery and let it tumble over the wall. A great shout went up from below.

"Let's get out of here, sir. The Frenchies are coming back. A passel of them."

Thomas looked around regretfully. How could he blow up the battery? The Frenchies had thrown all the loose gunpowder down the well. If only he'd thought to bring—

"Come *on*, sir!"

Next morning, Admiral Warren awoke to exclaim irritably, "Now what?" He hurried on deck. His jaw dropped. "The French are shelling their own positions!"

"It is Roebuck's battery, sir. He and his men stole a forty-two pounder out from under Frenchy's nose. They are shellin' the lovin' town!"

The men had worked all night building a carriage to hold the cannon. By morning they were gleefully firing away with Pepperrell's blessing. Thus the siege entered a second, more deadly phase.

The town was now being shelled without ceasing. A second battery was captured before the French crew had a chance to spike the cannons. Its guns were turned full force on the town. Within days the walls were breached in several places. Hardly a building had not been hit. Wails of women and children and bellows of frightened animals filled the flawless sky.

A message was sent to Chevalier Duchambon, commandant of the fortress, inviting his surrender. He stalled. A midnight raid of Indians and French dressed like Indians left a patrol of men from Massachusetts dead and mutilated. Pepperrell and Warren were outraged by such barbarism. Hearing of it, some men went out of control. Without orders, several frontiersmen formed their own raiding party. They returned hours later, grim faced and bloody, with a string of French scalps like seaweed on a line.

Some of Thomas's own men had participated. He felt horrified. This was not civilized war! This was hate. This was the kind of revenge Moses warned against.

Impatience grew for the war to end. Months of cold, illness, deprivation, and now degradation. Some talked incessantly of what they would do first when they raided the town. Brandy by the hogshead, French women, silks and laces and silverware. Thomas pleaded with his men to keep cool heads.

"Victory is surely ours. Remember that you are God-fearing men!"

One morning the batteries were rife with rumors that surrender was imminent. A private from headquarters company appeared with a message convening all battery officers at a meeting at Wolcott's tent.

"This is it," shouted Private Higgins, who had been Thomas's steward since Billy Lang went over the hill. "Betcha anything, sir, this is it!"

"Well, hold it in till I get back," said Thomas.

The French, perhaps realizing capitulation was near, fired that morning with maddened frenzy. Thomas stood with the other artillery and infantry officers, drinking coffee and listening as Wolcott outlined the positions he wanted their companies to take in town. Suddenly a terrific explosion rent the air. Thomas slammed his cup down.

"That came from my battery!" He and Sparhawk took off at a run, followed by the others. Black smoke belched from the battery. Screams of injured men pierced the air.

Thomas reached the battery and recoiled in horror. The French cannon had blown apart. Parts of bodies bloodied the battery grounds. "Lieutenant Roebuck," a voice cried.

"*Higgins?*" For a second Thomas couldn't see how anyone could be alive. Peter pulled him toward a tangled mass of smoking clothing. Higgins reached toward them with blackened arms. Thomas dropped to his side, and Higgins grabbed his overshirt. Thomas slipped an arm under the man's shoulders. He could feel warm blood soaking his sleeve. "What happened?"

"Sarge—sarge said let's give 'em a—a going-away present and so we—we double shotted the load—"

"Oh, no!" whispered Thomas as Higgins' eyes closed. He cradled the man in his arms.

"The medics are coming," said Peter.

"Get Parson Moody, too." All Thomas could think of, in that moment of death, was to thank God that it wasn't Billy Lang. He had promised Billy Lang to take care of him. If Billy hadn't deserted, this could have been he dying in his arms. Billy was safe with his "missus." Thank God, thank God, for that anyway.

During the day, Chevalier Duchambon capitulated. He asked only that he and his men be allowed to march out of Fort Louisbourg under their own banner, to surrender like gentlemen, according to the articles of war.

Pepperrell and Warren agreed. But the capitulation was held up an extra day when they could not agree to whom Duchambon should surrender. In the end, having suffered more and struggled more, Pepperrell won the day.

That was all the army won. Admiral Warren ordered that the French flag be kept flying over the town. In the weeks that followed, several vessels from France, including the heavily armed and heavily laden supply ships, sailed innocently into the harbor and were captured without a shot. Their cargo was immediately declared spoils of war: half to go to His Majesty, King George, half to the navy. Warren neither then nor later considered sharing the booty with the impoverished New England volunteer army.

In England the tidings of victory were received in late summer with astonishment and joy. But sober second thoughts reflected on the strength and mettle of colonists who seemed far to willing to act independently.

Meanwhile, on the day of the victory, jubilant English regulars and American volunteers had rushed to occupy a fort that had been considered impregnable and the town it supported. Pepperrell requested a prayer service held in the army-garrison chapel. To Thomas fell the task of locating Parson Moody.

He remembered seeing him march in with the troops, his old eyes ablaze with messianic zeal. Seeing a large crowd on the street, Thomas pushed his way to the front. About twenty women and children were being led from an artillery casemate. They had been hiding in the hot, airless shelter since yesterday. Thomas thought of his Gennie and was grateful that the war had been fought on French soil. Suddenly he recognized a head of golden curls. He was sure it was the gallant girl he had seen on the French ramparts, toasting her lover.

"Mademoiselle!"

She twisted around and shielded her eyes against the glare, until she found him.

He smiled. "Your lover is unharmed. I saw him."

She stared coldly for another moment, then flounced haughtily away with the others.

She had not understood. Thomas grinned. He could imagine what she thought he had said. He went on.

Thomas found Parson Moody at the Catholic church, axe in hand, panting from the accomplishment of his avowed task of chopping down the "altars of the Antichrist."

Standing before the men assembled a short time later, Moody foreswore his usual lengthy sermon, to mutter only, "Good Lord, we have so much to thank thee for, that time will be too short, and we must leave it for eternity. Bless our food and fellowship upon this joyful occasion, for the sake of Christ our Lord. Amen."

Thomas murmured his own amen and slipped outside. He saw that the general staff had found it necessary to post soldiers at the doors of the very houses they had planned to sack. Rumors of the town's poverty seemed to be true. Survivors among the inhabitants were begging for food.

Thomas thought of Private Higgins as he surveyed the broken town. There must be a better way. A holy war? No. Nothing holy about this war. Maybe not about any war. If the French loved God and their side loved God, why were they warring on each other, invoking the Holy One? He massaged his temple with a hand scorched by gunpowder. He reeked of sulfur.

"Thomas, look what I found for Father!" A jaunty Peter Sparhawk pounced on his friend. In his arms he carried a long, flat box. He opened it. "A brace of silver inlaid duelling pistols. Rather splendid for Father's trophy shelf, don't you think?"

"Why not?" said Thomas harshly and turned away.

·C·H·A·P·T·E·R·23·

ood morning, Goodwife Amos." Parson Cullers stepped inside quickly and pushed the door shut. "What a wind! It's going to be an early winter."

"Good morrow, Parson Cullers." Gennie stood behind the long counter in her husband's mercantile. Behind her were shelves she had spent all morning tidying. Neither dust nor wrinkle tainted the bolts of linen and wool goods, nor the spools of ribbon aligned above them.

Cullers glanced around and nodded approvingly. "You've brightened this place up. Even the hardware looks good." Then the frank blue eyes studied her. Marriage brought to many women such joy and contentment that they fairly radiated.

Gennie's brown eyes had lost their luster. Her long braid was coiled about her head in a severe coronet. His gaze traveled to the tapered fingers that rested on the counter. Had her hands always been so pale? Blue veins coursed under the translucent skin. She regarded him with a steady smile, her chin lifted.

"May I help you? My husband is over at the bank."

"I know. It is you I wanted to talk to."

The door burst open, and Goodman Amos scurried in. "Foul weather, Mrs. Amos. We'll get little trade today. Parson Cullers!"

Cullers thought he detected a defensive edge in his voice.

Goodman glanced swiftly at Gennie, then back at the parson. "Have you been here long?"

"Just arrived." He gave Amos a friendly, approving smile. "I was about to tell your wife how nice it is to come in and see a pretty, young face."

Amos parted with a grudging smile of propriety. "We mustn't spoil her."

Cullers caught an unfathomable look in Gennie's eyes before she moved away from her husband, to a shelf at the far end of the counter, where she commenced unpacking goods.

"What brings you out on such a day?" Amos asked, as if sensing he had intruded on a private conversation.

"I have news of an acquaintance of yours," Cullers said reluctantly, watching Gennie's back as she lifted a jar to a shelf above her head.

"Well, good or bad?" Goodman snapped. "You preachers can say more and less at the same time than anyone I know."

"It is about Thomas Roebuck. He's alive, Goodman."

The jar crashed to the floor and shattered. Gennie whirled. "I knew it! Alive! Praise God! Oh, Goodman, did you hear?" Her face was radiant.

Goodman eyed her coldly. "Madam, your joy is unseemly."

"But it is not, Goodman!" Cullers expostulated. "They were friends. We are all thankful his life has been spared."

Gennie's face was eloquent with questions. *How? How did such a dreadful mistake happen? Where is he now?*

To cover her confusion, she knelt to pick up the shards of glass.

Parson Cullers could hardly bear to look upon her. He doubted that Gennie had ever looked at Goodman with such joy. Seeing Goodman's face, he also knew with terrible premonition that the man would never forgive her.

Cullers laid a temporizing hand on Goodman's shoulder, which was shaking. "Come to the tavern, I'll buy you an ale. No sense telling my tale to one at a time."

His attempt to lighten the moment failed. Goodman shook off his hand. "I do not need to know any more. Go home, you clumsy woman! Someone else will clean it up! And do not stop to natter with females on the way!"

"Goodman . . . yes, Goodman." She left the glass where it lay.

"May I have the privilege of escorting you to your gate?"

"Thank you." Gennie reached for her bonnet and cloak.

Goodman scowled. He could hardly say nay. He turned away, not helping Gennie with her cloak.

Parson Cullers busied himself examining a barrel of axe handles. He feared that Gennie would suffer later if he displayed too much gallantry. But he could see his duty lay in talking some sense into Goodman Amos—and soon! The man got what he wanted. And it was certainly no secret that Gennie and Thomas had planned to marry.

Gennie walked decorously beside him as they proceeded down the street toward Amos' big white house a quarter of a mile away. How pretty she was! Like roses in the snow, her cheeks were suddenly blooming, as though Goodman's actions had no power to hurt her.

Impulsively she turned to him "Oh, Parson Cullers, tell me about Thomas! How is he? Was he wounded, perchance? When will he be home? I—I think I can almost bear my marriage to Mr. Amos, knowing that my . . . knowing that Thomas is safe. He *is* safe, isn't he?"

"Quite safe, as far as I know. He was not wounded at all." Parson

Cullers gazed at her in frank admiration. "I doubt your husband knows how lucky he is. You are quite a lady, Gennie. I have known about Thomas for two days, agonizing over telling you. You have been cruelly used." Briefly he recounted the tale brought by the coach driver from Boston.

Gennie stood quite still, her head bent. Then she faced him. "I will not think about that now. I will praise my Lord for Thomas's life," she said firmly. "As for my own . . ." She started walking again. A rueful smile crossed her lips. She was thinking of what Rosalind Hambleton had told her last year about marrying a rich old man. Goodman could not live forever. And Thomas had swore God meant for him to take care of her. She did not see how this could come to pass, but she was content to leave it in God's hands.

"Thomas is not coming back here," he said, trying to divine her thoughts. "Did you know his parents leased the farm? They have gone to Harper's Ferry, down in Virginia. Relatives there, I believe. Gennie, God has given you hard burdens . . ." Cullers removed his hat as they reached the gate. "If you ever need someone to talk with . . ."

"Thank you, Parson Cullers, I'll be all right," she said softly.

November 6, 1745. Such unbelieveable news today! Thomas *is* alive! Thank you, Lord. Whatever else my life has become, you have granted me a seed of happiness to cherish.

Goodman does not seem too pleased about the news.

Goodman Amos's lips compressed in anger. Softly he closed his wife's journal. No need to tell her he read French as well as she. He had been reading her daily entries since first discovering the journal—by accident, he told himself—going through his new wife's meager possessions after they returned from their weekend honeymoon in Philadelphia.

Goodman felt something else, too. He recalled his contempt at reading earlier entries. She despised him. That had been clear. Which made his petty cruelties even more satisfactory. She was getting what she deserved. Then why an uneasy knot in his insides? Was it because she had never lost her faith that Thomas was alive? Or was it her account of his promise to her? *God's* promise? Bah! Of course not. Any shrewd businessman knew better than to take religion too seriously.

Goodman placed the journal back in the chest where she kept her things. Well, this certainly justified his concern for her affairs. It was no more than a husband's duty, after all.

He looked at her, still asleep in their bed this cold morning, one forearm curled chastely under her head. A mass of rich chestnut locks spilled out over the pillow. Her rosy lips were parted slightly. Was that a smile? Was she dreaming of Roebuck?

Deceitful woman! He felt a rush of passion for her and anger because of it. He wrenched off his nightshirt and reached for the coverlet.

———————————————◆———————————————

Henri Zellaire was working in the barn later that same day, when he heard the buckboard. That would be Marie Therese returning from helping to sew a trousseau for a coming wedding. He had permitted her to join the sewing circle, hoping that the gaiety and rush of excitement attending the wedding would soften her attitude toward him, so that she would consent to marry him. Since her daughter's marriage, Marie Therese had made no secret of her displeasure with him. He was fairly certain that Gennie had not told her the real reason she suddenly agreed to marry Goodman, for it was unlike Marie Therese to keep woes to herself! Why had he this uncomfortable feeling, then, each time they spoke of Gennie and Goodman?

He leaned on his rake, anticipating her coming into the barn with all the news, while his son Jean unhitched the team. Instead it was Jean who came in.

" 'Lo, Papa," he said, leading the team. Jean was almost up to his father's shoulder now, a slender redhead with a likable air.

"Hello, son. Did Madame Harmonie come back with you?"

"Yes, sir. Papa, she didn't say one word all the way home. She acted right put out."

Thoughtfully, Henri pulled at his chin. Then he leaned his rake against a post and went to wash up.

Minutes later he was standing outside her bedroom door. He heard muffled sobs. He knocked. "Madame? Are you all right?"

Since her final refusal, a cold truce had existed between them and a mutual pretence before the children that nothing was amiss.

The sobbing abated.

"Marie Therese?" A note of concern crept into his voice. Gently he tried the door. Swiftly she rose to meet him, her back straight and her chin defiantly raised. He was almost afraid to ask why she was crying.

"Well, what is it?" he said roughly.

How could she have had so little judgment that she actually loved this man, who had allowed greed to sour his good Christian nature! Oh, if it were not for the children—"Thomas Roebuck is alive."

Color drained from Zellaire's face. "Alive?" he croaked.

"No one in the regiment knew we thought he was dead, until they returned from Louisbourg. General Roger Wolcott found a letter from Mr. Roebuck, wanting to know how his son died."

"But—"

"His steward got drunk the night before they left, stole Thomas's coat, and deserted. They think it must have been he who was killed."

Each word flung at him dropped like a hot coal in his mind. Thomas alive! Then he, Henri Zellaire, had broken his word. And what had he lost! He remembered confessing to Thomas his own love for Marie Therese. How prophetic those words, said in what he thought later was a moment of weakness, when he realized that his love for the mother was linked inextricably to Thomas's love for the daughter.

Henri backed out and closed the bedroom door. He stumbled downstairs and into his workshop. The two slaves he had acquired from Goodman Amos glanced around curiously at him, then went back to work, one operating the forge, the other beating a metal hasp into shape.

"You are free," he said hoarsely.

Now they stopped work and turned to stare at him.

He glared at them, struggling for control. "I am freeing you both. I will sign the papers today. You can get jobs in town, or you can go back where you came from. You can stay here until you decide. Go outside. Leave me. Go work in the barn!" He shooed them outside as if they were pestery children.

Go, go, go . . . Oh, God, God! Unwillingly he thought of the over-bearing attitude of Goodman Amos toward Gennie, the dozens of little ways in which he showed the citizens of Germantown his contempt for his new wife. He thought of her fortitude. No one, not even from rumors by Amos' servants, had heard her utter a word against him. Yet her unhappiness was plain to see, to anyone who had known her before.

Why? Why had Amos insisted on marrying Gennie if it clearly made even himself unhappy? No one treated a wife as he was treating Gennie, if he were pleased and proud of her.

Oh, blessed Savior! How much was on his soul! Zellaire prostrated himself on the dirt floor of the workshop and wept.

ou have a lady love, I seem to remember."

"Yes, sir," Thomas grinned fatuously. "She's indentured, but her master has promised to free her to marry me as soon as I get back."

Roger Wolcott rose from his desk and paced around the spacious library of the Sparhawk mansion. After their return from Louisbourg, the elder Sparhawk had invited the general staff to be guests at his home until their forces were officially disbanded. Thomas was staying there also, as Peter's guest.

Wolcott picked up a letter from the desk. "This letter was written some time ago. It seems that for a time your father was under the impression you were deceased."

"Deceased! It can't be!"

"No, now wait, Thomas, don't go off half cocked. It's been cleared up; headquarters sent a reply a month ago, before Christmas. Just wanted you to be aware of it. Someone wearing your coat was slain, presumably by Indians. Your letter to your father was found and forwarded with the coat. Headquarters immediately dispatched a messenger to Harper's Ferry—"

"Where?"

"Yes, they left Germantown. It's all in the letter," Wolcott said a trifle impatiently. "Thomas, I want you to stay with me."

Harper's Ferry! Heavenly Father! Thomas pictured his father, unable to bear staying where Thomas had grown up, perhaps believing himself the reason Thomas was slain, because he had encouraged him to volunteer.

". . . You've proved a resourceful and courageous officer, and we want to commission you as a scout . . ."

And Gennie! What if she had also heard the rumor? He had to get back there as soon as possible. And what if Zellaire—he didn't trust him for a minute where there was money to be made.

"Roebuck! Are you listening?"

"Sir, I have to—"

"Hear me out." It was an order.

Thomas riveted his gaze on his superior.

"We know pretty much where the French have their forts along the Lakes. But from the fur post at Le Detroit, they are also moving southeast into the Ohio. The latest intelligence is that they are trying to lure La Demoiselle, the chief of the Miamis, into their fold. We want you to go, not as a military man, but as a trapper, first to Le Detroit, then down to the Ohio territory as our emissary to La Demoiselle. You will be given presents for him. We'll give you such maps as we have and hope you can improve upon them when you return." Wolcott struck a confident stance and challenged him to reply.

Thomas forced himself to think about his offer. He shook his head, a slow grin breaking over his face. "Sir, it's no use. Right now all I can think about is my 'lady love,' as you call her. I must see her."

"Very well. Take a month."

Again Thomas shook his head. "I do thank you for the honor," he said firmly, "but I reckon I've had enough fighting. I want to be a farmer, like my pa. Settle in the Ohio valley somewhere."

"Consider, Roebuck. This would give you a chance to explore those very lands! Do not refuse me yet. Take your leave, you've earned it. Send me a message when you've decided."

"Yes, sir, I'll do that, sir." Thomas extended his hand, and Wolcott shook it firmly.

"And give my regards to—"

"Gennie, sir."

"Yes, Gennie."

January, 1746. I am so humiliated. Mama came to see me today, and I had the servants tell her I did not wish to see her. I do not know what it is that I am doing that is so bad, 'pon heaven I do not! I have struggled to be a good, dutiful wife and to show my husband honor. Yet Goodman says I am wicked and that is why he must beat me. I have been stiff and sore for two days. I am ashamed to let Mama see me until my bruises have faded. She is bound to think I have done something to disgrace her.

Father, I pray thee to make me with child. Then Goodman will leave me at peace! And surely, Father, he will not beat me then, when I am carrying his child.

General Wallingham looked even more shrunken to Thomas as he swung through the door of the Crown and Rose tavern in Hartford. The public room was full and Wallingham himself helping out, ladling hot cider to his customers.

He glanced up with a welcoming smile as the coach passengers trooped in. As he spied Thomas his jaw gaped and the ladle of hot cider clattered to the polished floor. "Master Roebuck! But you are dead, lad!"

A frightful silence descended on the public room. The supping men twisted about to see the stranger who was thought dead. They saw a handsome young officer wrapped in a heavy, fawn wool coat and wearing a black tricorn sporting the colors of the Connecticut regiment.

"Upon my soul. Oh, my. Oh, my." Wallingham left the maids to mop up the spilled cider. He hastened to Thomas, stretching out both hands, feeling his arms through the layers of heavy clothing, and peering up into his face. "It is Thomas Roebuck, is it not, of the Germantown post road?"

"You know it is, General," laughed Thomas, anxious to put him at ease and turn those curious eyes back to their supper plates. "The rumors of my death were somewhat premature."

"Come with me." Ignoring his other guests, General Wallingham literally pulled Thomas through the tiny lobby, and up the stairs to his private sitting room. Beckoning his guest to the only chair, he withdrew a letter from a mahogany secretary and adjusted his glasses.

"Look, general, if it's my—"

Wallingham was not to be diverted. He shook his head and produced a clucking sound. "Thomas, my dear young friend, this pains me greatly. I . . ." The old man swallowed and gave him the letter.

The letter was from Henri Zellaire, in which he told how William Roebuck had come to town one day to arrange a memorial service for his oldest son, killed in an Indian raid. A letter from Thomas, bearing rusty stains of dried blood, was delivered inside a letter written in French, describing the circumstances by which the Frenchman had come into possession of the letter and describing the green coat from which it had been taken.

Thomas thrust the letter back at Wallingham. "Yes, I know all this, sir. Headquarters notified—"

Tears ran down the old general's face. He pushed the letter away as if it were plagued. "But ye should also know that Henri speaks of a girl, a French girl. You and she were courting. She was so overcome by news of your death that she agreed to be married to Goodman—"

Thomas heard a great roar in his ears. "No! No!"

"Thomas, lad, they are already married. You must pray for strength and wisdom." Wallingham shifted uncomfortably. "I must get back to my guests. Stay. Stay the night. Please." With obvious relief, he escaped.

"Why?" Thomas bellowed at the closing door. "O, God, why?"

Thomas did not sleep that night. His knees were burned raw as he prayed in agony. *Gennie . . . Gennie . . . How could she?* He seethed with anger. *So little faith!* Hadn't he promised? Hours later the anger fell way to tears as he sobbed in the privacy of the room Wallingham had insisted on giving him, grieving for what was lost forever.

Night paled. His reason exhausted, Thomas lashed out at a cruel Providence for what he saw as betrayal. Had not he volunteered to defend the true faith against Papists? Had not he fought God's own war? God at least should have kept those he held dear safe whilst he was about His business! God was guilty of a breach of faith!

As dawn crested the sill, Thomas threw himself on the eider-down and pulled part of it over his frozen limbs. He felt calm now, at least for a time. Providence never closed one avenue without opening another. Wolcott had wanted him as a military scout. Very well. He would still be serving his land and his God, even if God . . . He could not bear to go home now.

Gennie must have been married not long after that fateful fishing trip when his greatcoat and Billy Lang had both disappeared. He remembered the unbearable golden beauty of that afternoon. . . .

When he heard the servants up and about in the kitchen below, Thomas washed himself, combed and retied his black hair, and descended the stairs. He called for pen and paper. He wrote a letter to his family, ate breakfast, thanked General Wallingham, and returned by the morning stage to Boston.

Wolcott smoked in silence while Thomas poured out his heart and soul. Finally he laid a hand on the young man's shoulder. Thomas remained with his head buried in his hands.

"It is a cruel thing you are living through, Roebuck. But God will use this tragedy in your life to his glory. Don't ask me how. . . . But already I can see it working in you. Older and more experienced men would have taken to drink or gone back and made life hell for everyone. You have chosen the path of self-discipline and righteousness."

Thomas knew only that he had done what had to be done. It would have served no good purpose to see Gennie and increase his own agony. Maybe she was happy now.

pril 14, 1746. I am so happy! Goodman has not touched me for a week, not since I told him I am with child. He brought home half a length of yellow silk from the store and permitted me to make a dress to wear to church on Easter. I was able to see Mama and little Jean and Carrie and the other children. Mama and M. Zellaire have not married. Goodman does not leave me alone with Mama to inquire the reason.

M. Zellaire insisted that we accompany them back home for a proper Easter Sunday dinner, and Goodman did not dare refuse. While we were at the farm, he treated me as befitting a wife. Oh, I wish that he would treat me as well all the time. Then, blessed Savior, I would not complain about my lot. Mama was made happy by the news of our blessed event. She believes I have forgotten Thomas and am enjoying my wedded state.

I shall never tell her otherwise, for it is not in her power to change anything. Only thee, Lord! If Goodman takes up again with his fists and his straps, I shall pray thee to take me home.

August 4, 1746. Sweet Jesus, I am so sick I can barely move. How foolish I was to think that carrying his child would save me from Goodman's moral determination to beat the wickedness out of my flesh. Sometimes when he is finished, he cries and begs my forgiveness. Only God can forgive him! The servants disappear when they hear my cries. Does no one care? Surely, surely, his grown sons, Parson Cullers—someone—knows what he is doing!

Hell cannot be worse than this.

December 12, 1746. The baby has not kicked for nearly a month. Oh, I am so frightened. What if my child is stillborn? Please, blessed Savior, let it be all right!

January 20, 1747. Praise God! My precious baby lives! His head is misshapen. Mama and Rosalind both say that is nothing to worry about; Benjamin is only four days old. Mama says his little red face looks just like mine did when I was born. I have no milk yet, but Mama says soon. I worry, though. What if Goodman's blows have permanently injured my breasts?

My Lord Jesus, I have failed to make my husband happy. I freely acknowledge this. But I know I am worth something. I know that you value each soul as a person. I do not believe that you mean for me to be abused so shamefully and needlessly.

Wicked thoughts come unbidden. What paradise it would have been to be married to my love, my Thomas.

As long as I have my beautiful baby I am determined to be happy for his, Benjamin's, sake.

February 25, 1747. Oh I think I shall die of unhappiness. The bitterness of the cold outside is as nothing compared to the hatred in my heart. Something is dreadfully wrong with Benjamin. He does not hold down milk well, but spits up most of it. Goodman blames it upon the poisonous quality of my milk. Benjamin cries so piteously it wrenches my insides. It drives me to distraction, for nothing I do for him seems to make a difference! His head is still misshapen, though I press it gently each day. But worse, one eye has no white, but a frame of blood red around the orb. Goodman says he is a devil child. God forgive me, but I know it is Goodman's fault! My hatred of him is unremitting. I will never love him. Never!

Goodman leaves us alone now. He cannot bear to look upon our child as I, alas, cannot bear to leave it.

February 26, 1747. A storm is raging outside. It has snapped off the little plum tree I planted outside the nursery. Goodman is now threatening to have me declared a witch. He says Benjamin is proof enough. He says if I try to spread lies, he will make me confess in church that I cast a spell upon him, and when he had made me his wife, I birthed a monster.

No one will come between a man and his wife. I know that now. I tried to tell Parson Cullers, but Goodman was all smiles and pulled me away. Goodman knows better than to leave me alone with Mama. He could not prevent her presence when the baby was born, but he left the room only when I could not possibly speak.

March 14, 1747. It is starting again. There was blood in my milk today when I nursed the baby. Goodman will never change. His hatred of me has increased twelvefold since Benjamin's birth. Daily I fear that he will harm the child. I see it in his eyes. The servants pity me, but they are powerless and in great fear of him.

I have conceived a plan to end it. I am frightened to see it to the end. *Le bon Dieu,* hear my cries.

he trapper's pipe had gone out. Balancing one ice-encrusted boot against a granite boulder, he leaned his flintlock against his knee and stripped off a mitten. He fumbled for tobacco and tamped his pipe. His blue eyes gleamed briefly as he flamed the tobacco. He drew on the pipe, and the light left his eyes again. The wind whistled off the straits. He gazed across the ice floes drifting silently by, to the French outpost on the opposite shore.

Fort Pontchartrain du Detroit was a long, rectangular stockade with full bastions at the corners. The busiest of all French fur trading outposts, Le Detroit, nestled in full security within the fort's walls. The land outside the stockade was speckled with fires, moth-bright beacons of warmth among scattered birch and sod huts that looked like oversized brown beetles.

In this zone of truce, the French, as was their custom, offered protection to all tribes in the territory, in order to secure first claim on their furs. Tribal courtesy and sense of fairness demanded that if they accepted one, they honored the other. Thomas Roebuck marveled that they succeeded so well. Frenchy neither paid as well as the English nor had the variety of well-made goods to offer in trade. During the frigid afternoon, he had watched the comings and goings of many tribesmen hauling sleds heaped with furs.

Thomas turned his gaze to the north. Over Lake Saint Clair, the clouds were breaking up. One hundred miles south, spring was already coaxing blossoms from the buds. As he had trekked north through the Ohio valley, checking traps, making notes for his maps, and recording movements of Indians and French, he had moved back into a winter of blacks and grays and whites.

As if to compensate, the sun remained longer in the sky, heralding long, pewter-colored twilights. This vast territory was all claimed by Connecticut—"west to the Great Western Ocean," was how Roger Wolcott put it, when Thomas had asked him about it last year, after his first year as scout.

The first year, Thomas ranged up and down the Ohio, trapping furs and later selling them. He had visited La Demoiselle and established an initial friendly climate. He had charted maps for Wolcott. The second year, he ventured into territory claimed by the French.

Boldly he set his lines among the traps of French coureurs de bois, along the streams and rivers connecting Fort Pontchartrain with French outposts on the Maumee, the Scioto and the Miami rivers.

The light was nearly gone now. And his job here was done, his notes completed. At dawn he would skirt the southwestern edge of Lake Erie and head for the English outpost at Onondaga, south of Lake Ontario.

He cupped the glowing embers of his pipe so that it could not be seen across the straits. From habit, his thoughts returned to Gennie. The trees around him suddenly reminded him of bare swords, piercing the earth. The pain was a dull ache now. He welcomed it. He nourished it. It was better than forgetfulness.

Perhaps at Onondaga new orders from Wolcott awaited him. If not, what then? He had to go home sometime.

———————— • ————————

All Germantown knew that Goodman Amos had quarreled with the pastor of the French Reformed Church over his son's christening. Amos had insisted that Benjamin was too sickly to be taken outside. The christening and baptism must be done at home, privately.

Parson Cullers adamantly refused. The law is God's, he said. If it is his will that Benjamin be baptised, then he will surely keep him healthy for it! Cullers set time and date and forbade any more discussion. Even Amos was not brave enough to disobey.

Every new soul born in this sparse and beautiful country was a cause for celebration. Most of the townfolk attending little Benjamin's christening came that Sunday evening in a spirit of giving thanks. But some came too from malicious curiosity, eager to glimpse the rumored monster birthed by Gennie Harmonie Amos.

Rosalind Hambleton did not attend. Though the evening was chilly, as early June is prone to be, she hitched her mule to the cart used on midwife calls and proceeded into town on a different errand.

She approached the church from the rear, remaining in the deep shadows fifty yards away. A square of light appeared then vanished; a muffled figure, appearing then reappearing, melted away from the church.

Rosalind slipped down and went to meet the figure. When they met, the two women clasped arms around a swaddled bundle. Soon all three were huddled on the cart seat and moving into the shadows.

"You lucky it cold out, no one notice you got on so many clo'es," Rosalind said to Gennie half an hour later, critically watching her nurse Benjamin in the safety and warmth of Rosalind's cabin. A wonder she had any milk at all.

Life was slow in Germantown. Rumors reached everywhere. And those that had reached Rosalind's ears about Mr. Amos' scandalous treatment of his young wife had caused her to nod her head knowingly at the evil of the world. Never would it have occurred to her to do anything about it—it was just the way things were—except that one of Amos' servants had brought a message from Gennie, begging her help.

She was watched continually in the house, Gennie had told her. But at the church, Amos could not possibly watch her all the time without creating suspicion. Gennie was determined to leave him. Surely God had not intended his people to be slaves!

Now Gennie reached over and caressed Rosalind's hand where it clasped her knee. "I shall never be able to thank you," she said softly. "I didn't know if you would come. I didn't know if I could truly slip away!" Gennie laughed. Now that she had actually taken that first step, she felt giddy and frightened at the same time.

"I told Goodman that Benjamin had just filled his napkin. I was afraid he would tell me to have the servant change it. But everyone was coming up offering congratulations, so I just said I'd slip into Parson Cullers' study and change it. And, well, out the back door and here I am!"

The ride back to Rosalind's cabin had been almost anticlimactic. Rosalind was certain no one would suspect where she had been or even that she had been out. The two women sat in the cosy comfort of the fire and grinned happily at each other.

Rosalind said, "I got you pretty good supply dried meat and biscuit. Now. You follow the road on in to Philadelphia, and you come to the Delaware River. And you keep to this side of it, hear? And just head south. To your right. Keep the river on your left. Pretty soon you be out of Pennsylvania. Ain't no one likely to send you back, you get that far. Where you headin' again?"

"Should I tell you? I don't want you to jeopardize your soul with a lie."

Rosalind threw her a wry grin. As if helping a man's wife to run away wasn't jeopardizing enough!

Gennie read the look and smiled. "Harper's Ferry. His parents will take care of me."

"Thomas Roebuck again, eh?"

"Always," Gennie said firmly.

"Yeah, well, if he don't show up, you git some meat on your

bones so you be pretty again an' git yourself another man. Heap o' fine men around and ain't a whole lot o' women."

Neither mentioned the fact that traveling on foot with a sickly five-month-old in these last, unpredictable weeks of spring could be tantamount to a death sentence.

Gennie's eyes grew luminous with gratitude. "I'll be all right," she insisted. "We are safe in the hands of our Lord. Hasn't he delivered us so far?" She hugged Benjamin tenderly. "Just knowing that . . ." she finished the thought in her mind: that Goodman will never again get his brutal hands on either of them filled her with tremendous strength.

Rosalind seemed to sense in Gennie's desperation her willingness to die to escape the hell life had become. After a pause, she said, "One thing, Gennie Amos, stay away from Indians, hear? A woman is not worth a heap o' ashes to them. 'Les they think you a runaway slave. Then they takes real good care of you, 'caise there's likely a bounty."

Rosalind's words fell on deaf ears as Gennie gave in to overwhelming tiredness. "Rosalind, I must sleep for two or three hours. Will it be safe?"

"Don't see why not."

———◆———

"An' the next morning, 'bout two hours before the cock crew, she got herself and that baby ready," Rosalind was to tell her friends later. "We done prayed together, and Lord, if that weren't the strongest prayin' I ever done in my life. See, she didn't have nobody but her Jesus to protect her. 'Caise that Mr. Amos, he was a evil man. A evil man! And he woulda kilt her for sure."

Goodman Amos, in the uproar following the discovery that his wife was missing, had gone alternately redder of face and puffier of breath. His loud expostulation of Indians on the warpath diverted no one. Tribes in eastern Pennsylvania had been peaceable for twenty years.

By the end of the second day, stories with a grain of truth began to circulate. On the third day, Marie Therese paid a visit to Parson Cullers, who admitted that he had suspected Goodman Amos was abusing his wife and possibly his child. But it was not an outsider's place to interfere with a man's discipline in his own home.

Firmly Marie Therese persuaded Parson Cullers they should pay a call on Goodman Amos, to discover a reason why a frail young woman with a sickly baby should suddenly run away.

Goodman watched them, through the parlor curtains of his fine house, panting in funny little gasps. By the time a servant admitted his visitors to the parlor, Goodman Amos lay on the floor. His limbs were still jerking, but he longer cared how he appeared to his guests.

Gennie, meanwhile, walked confidently and steadily to the outskirts of Philadelphia, arriving shortly after dawn. Her spirit was singing in the pale, misty June sunlight. Benjamin had slept most of the way, but was awake now, his eyes watching his mother's face with trusting serenity. A quick smile lighted her face as she discovered his attention. She drew off the road, seeking but not finding a sheltered place that was also free from dew, and settled finally on her cloak. She laid Benjamin beside her.

Later, after she had nursed the baby and eaten and rested a little, she arranged her bundles over her shoulders and gathered Benjamin again in her arms. Soon she came to a confusing array of water. Was this the Delaware? Or was it only an offshoot? Should she cross the bridge or turn south here? "Lord Jesus, tell me what to do," she whispered. "Well, Benjamin," she said, her voice sounding very loud in the stillness, "the sooner out of Pennsylvania, the better. I guess we will turn south here."

By midmorning the river began veering southwest. The well-traveled road she had been following seemed to be narrowing. But perhaps it was just that the foliage was thicker here. She plunged on.

No wonder that riders, coming two and three days later, egged on by goodwives filled with indignation and by their own stricken consciences, missed her.

"Apoplexy, suffered in a paroxym of grief, has taken brother Goodman Amos," intoned Parson Cullers that same day. And then, after an hour of eulogies at his funeral, the subject of Goodman and Gennie Amos was dropped almost as quickly as the clods of earth that fell on his grave. No one felt very comfortable with the alternative. She was, after all, his wife. Who were they to interfere?

Only Marie Therese, Henri Zellaire, and the children grieved. Rosalind, though not daring to reveal her part in Gennie's escape, laid anxious hints abroad in town, whereabouts she'd look if on'y she was a man.

·C·H·A·P·T·E·R·27·

he sun was warm at her back and Gennie's spirits gay. They had both slept well last night and the night before. All day she followed the rushing, rain-swollen stream without encountering another person. Nor had she crossed any other paths, much less a post road. She began to wonder if she had missed the landmarks that Rosalind had told her to watch for, that would tell her she was out of Pennsylvania. Nevertheless her heart sang. She was free! Benjamin was safe. Now that they were away from Amos, she knew her dear Lord Jesus would heal her son. Softly she hummed a hymn from her childhood.

In midafternoon she collapsed, with a breathy laugh, on a bed of pliant ferns, to rest and feed Benjamin. Perhaps she would soon come upon the property of a charitable and pious farmer who would allow her to work there in exchange for room and board for a few days. She was strong now. Why, she could work as hard as any woman . . .

Gennie awoke with a start. Goodness! She had fallen asleep. Benjamin's mouth had fallen away from her breast. His lips were sweetly parted as he dozed, slightly sour of breath, still bubbly with warm milk. She hoped he had taken enough. She felt his stomach, thinking of the bulging bellies of puppies after nursing. He didn't feel full. And his ribs still looked like a birdcage. She frowned. Maybe real babies just didn't look full the way puppies did. Yes. That was all. With care she bound a fresh napkin on him, rinsed his soiled one in the stream, and tied one end of it to her bundle, to flap dry as she walked.

While she slept, large, puffy clouds had begun to pile up in thunderheads, tumbling swiftly across the sky, dispelling warmth, smelling of rain. Now she noticed her path widening again. That meant sooner or later she would come across a farm, if not a settlement.

A herd of deer grazed on the far side of a meadow, perhaps half a mile away. She paused to watch, conscious suddenly of birdsong, of calls and whistles of nest builders. Eagerly her eyes scanned the trees, knowing what she was looking for and finding it: a tree—it could even be an apple tree—gloriously cloaked in white blossoms. Praise God! What a beautiful land, just like their farm in Le Havre. Surely goodness and mercy *were* following her!

For several more days, Gennie traveled steadily southwestward. Harper's Ferry was firmly fixed in her mind. She had located it among the other names written in India ink on the watercolored map in Goodman's library. She had memorized the names of several settlements in northern Maryland and Virginia. Sometimes she chanted these names to the rhythm of nursery rhymes, to keep up her spirits. Sometimes she imagined the surprise of Mr. and Mrs. Roebuck when she arrived with Benjamin. But they would see that she was a capable worker and able to pay for her keep.

She imagined the glorious morning when Thomas Roebuck rode home. She saw him framed in the doorway, the light behind him as it had been when he visited her at Zellaire's farm, saw his eyes lighting up and following her as she moved about the room. Maybe he was already home! He would protect her. He would never let Goodman have her again. She would love him and honor him as long as she lived.

"Come, Benjy, Mama's precious," murmured Gennie, hitching him more securely in the sling on her hip and setting off again. The stream she was following plunged directly across a wide sloping meadow, but Gennie, fearing marshes, skirted it, planning to meet it again on the opposite side. Benjamin was such a good baby. Lately he seldom cried, but slept longer and longer. Healing. That was what he was doing, healing. Comforted, Gennie lifted her face to the wind and went on.

Within an hour, though not yet sunset, clouds smothered the sky with a heavy cloak of gray pocked with black. Gennie quickened her pace. Darkness fell just as she found unexpected shelter in a shallow cave. "Thank you, Lord," she murmured, creeping within.

To a mighty boom of thunder, the rains danced outside her cave. Noise and lightning jousted in the sky. In another place Gennie would have found it fascinating. Yet, she was not particularly frightened. She had beef and biscuit for another week, if she was careful; ripe berries were plentiful; and water was everywhere. Benjamin was still not nursing well, but a night's sleep would restore her milk and his appetite, she was certain. So it was with a great outpouring of gratitude that she offered her prayers, more concerned for Mama than herself. Had Rosalind told her, she wondered?

Each time the grasping fingers of fear reached from the dark corners of the cave to taunt her, she met them with God's word. She and Benjy were his lambs. The Shepherd would not let them be lost. They were His sparrows. Even the sparrow finds a home, and the swallow a nest for herself, where she may raise her young without fear. Thus comforted, Gennie slept.

Benjamin was more lethargic than he had ever been the morning of the third day after the storm. Gennie crept outside. Her limbs felt stiff. The sky was a deep azure, as though the storm had been but a dream. Their footpath was obliterated, but the sunlight was strong and warm. Gennie could hardly wait to get going again. She came back in the cave.

"Wake up, little one. Time to eat." She had to pinch Benjy's cheek to arouse him. At last, whining weakly in protest, he accepted her nipple. After a long moment, in which he seemed to be making up his mind, his little cheeks pulled in and he began to nurse. Watching him, Gennie felt a nameless dread hovering in the shadows. Her breathing grew shallow. No! No. My Shepherd is with me. She thrust the shadows away.

Gennie lost count of the days. She had seen no white persons. And dutifully she hid from Indians, families and hunters alike. One morning she realized the countryside was subtly changed from the rolling farmlands around Germantown. Outcrops of rock jutted erratically, amid rushing streams and downed trees that were criss-crossed like sticks, as if felled by floods. She gazed helplessly at the vista. No road, no path. Nor had there been for days, she realized dully. She had just taken her bearings each morning and walked . . .

Suddenly, from the corner of her eye, she glimpsed a patch of bright green amid the browns and sooty greens of the forest. She deposited her bundles and Benjamin at the foot of some boulders and scaled a few feet, pulling herself with both arms over the top boulder so she could see. Her heart leaped joyously.

Below, set back from a rocky streambed, was a single cabin. The green she had seen was a small vegetable garden. As she watched, a huge woman in long red-and-black skirt moved in and out of the rows with some sort of hoe. She heard a male voice calling. A young man, perhaps the woman's son, emerged from the cabin.

Praise the Lord! She was saved! Gennie was seized by a dizziness so intense that she could barely make it down the rocks.

Benjamin's body felt like a bundle of wet wash when she lifted him in her arms. She pulled the blanket away from his face. It looked so still. She touched his cheek. It was chapped and felt like limestone. His bowels had run freely the last few days. He had hardly nursed at all. Her breasts were enlarged and tender from the unrelieved quantities.

Gennie thrust aside the blankets and felt Benjy's limbs. So cold! She chafed them. He would not open his eyes. She pleaded. She begged. Tears streamed from her eyes. "Benjamin," she whispered. "My Benjamin."

ndrew Montour had been educated by nuns at the Ursuline convent at Quebec. His mother was an Erie, his father French. He never remembered his father, who had returned to France at the conclusion of his military service.

Andrew's mixed parentage was not held against him, and he was educated as thoroughly as the legal offspring of the few French families who elected to remain in the New World. He had more than justified the liberal attention to his upbringing. Montour spoke several languages and dialects. He was adept at assuming identities of foreign tribes. Thus, at the English fort at Onondaga, in August 1747, he was temporarily a Seneca, of the Iroquois nation, and friendly to the English.

Montour strode boldly out the open gates of the English stockade, intending by all indications to hunt deer. Once concealed in the brush, however, his pose dropped. He altered direction. Minutes later he was squatting in a small clearing next to a heavily bearded trapper.

"The man you seek was there four days. He ate with the officers, but did not speak often. I learned that a message was given to him from a man named Roger Wolcott."

"*Bien!*" exclaimed the other man. "And naturally you availed yourself—"

"Naturally. When he was asleep. He is to go to the land of the Miamis. He is to speak to La Demoiselle. There was more, but not time to read it."

If Montour had expected his words to elicit outrage, he was disappointed. The Frenchman merely reached inside his clothing and scratched at his fleas.

Montour sucked in his copper cheeks. "That is not all. During good light, he made maps from many notes. And he traded his furs for pounds sterling. A hard trader, m'sieu," Montour added with respect in his voice. "But not a happy man."

The Frenchman turned to him with interest. "No?"

"Smoke too much. Too much alone. No woman."

The Frenchman nodded. He sprang to his feet. His build was wiry, his skin tanned to a shade that would credit a Spaniard. His stained parka had seen better days.

"You have done well, Montour." Reaching into his pack he presented Montour with a packet containing a pound of the finest French tobacco. "Let us go."

Montour appeared puzzled.

"To the man, Montour. It is time we met."

"But he has left the fort."

"Left?"

"Yesterday."

Now the Frenchman swore a steady volley of oaths. Rapidly he began stuffing his possessions back in his pack.

Montour looked troubled. "Three Senecas also left. I think they were following him."

"Why?"

Montour shrugged. "The silver. I did not think it mattered. You have the information you paid for."

Thomas threw himself on the ground and drank from the stream alongside his horse and mule. He was nearly exhausted. For three days he had known he was being followed. He had pressed the animals as hard as he dared. And then yesterday, in a fool-stupid mistake, he had not watched what he was doing. While he was cleaning an infected sore in its ear, the mule had rewarded him by stepping on his foot.

At first it had not bothered him. Through his thick boot, he scarcely felt it. But this morning his foot was swollen and sporting angry shades of purple. It was impossible to draw the boot over it. In the end he had pulled on three thick stockings and bound his foot and ankle in a beaver fur.

His trackers must have sensed their advantage. They were careless now, shouting back and forth to each other, as if waging warfare on the mind of their quarry. Why risk the magic power of his flintlock? All they need do was run him to ground. They seemed to know where he was headed. On foot, he knew, they could catch him easily. Yet he could not remain indefinitely in the saddle.

If memory served, a small hunting camp of the Hurons lay an hour's ride ahead. Thomas tried to reason like his pursuers. If they had followed him from Onondaga, they knew he was allied with the English. Therefore they would expect him to avoid a Huron camp.

If they believed this, they might separate and meet again beyond the camp. They would not expect him to backtrack. Perhaps he could trick them.

Thomas pulled the animals into a thick copse of trees on the banks of a swiftly descending stream. The roar of plunging white water would disguise any small sounds from the animals.

He eased himself off the horse and tethered both beasts securely. The horse shifted, causing him to move his weight momentarily to his wounded foot. He gasped with pain and shoved his face into the horse's flank. He lowered himself to the mossy ground. Providence was testing him!

He'd eaten on the run, out of saddlebags, until his store was exhausted. He had not dared use his gun to bring down game. He eyed the rushing waters ruefully. Oh, for the paw of a bear! He would set a trap.

Hopping awkwardly on his good foot, Thomas assembled a trap from the pack on the mule. He checked his gun. Using it as a cane, he set off upstream—away, he hoped, from his pursuers—seeking an inviting pool in which to lower the trap. Moist, velvet shadows shrouded the banks of the stream. He grew absorbed in his task. Suddenly he heard a low crow of triumph. He whirled. A musket was aimed at his belly. He stared at the grinning face above it.

"You!"

"You!" the Frenchman echoed. He lowered his gun.

"You weasel, you pond scum, you barnyard filth!" Thomas croaked. "Tell me why I should not kill you!"

"Because it is I who have the drop on you, *mon ami*."

"You stole my furs."

"Listen to the young man who drank all my good brandy." The Frenchman glanced around sharply, his quick, black eyes darting across the stream and behind Thomas. Then he said loudly, "I thought you would never come. I was about to break camp and tell La Demoiselle you were not coming. He is sending us an escort."

Thomas stared. What in the name of Providence was he talking about? It *was* Captain Jack, the coureur de bois encountered nearly three years ago in Pennsylvania, but who was he? How did he know so much about him?

The Frenchman's glance shifted from the trap in Thomas's hand to the flintlock used like a staff, easing the weight from his lame foot. He lowered his voice. "Your three friends are not far. Can you make it to the Huron camp?"

Thomas hissed, "I've no intention of going to the Huron camp. My friends, as you call them, know that. By this time they will be after me beyond the camp."

"That may be. But they, too, know where you are going. They

will ambush you before you reach the Miamis. For your silver, you see," the Frenchman jibed.

Thomas gripped his temples between thumb and fingers. Was the man in league with his trackers, then? "Who are you?" he said quietly.

"My name is Etienne Harmonie. Captain Jack is a name I was saddled with when I first set foot in Quebec, do not ask me why."

"Harmonie!" An image of Gennie leaped to his mind. He searched the dark face, the black eyes, trying to discern some likeness.

"Gennie is my little cousin. And if you are Thomas Roebuck, I am he who found your greatcoat. Bought it, actually. Cost me more than it was worth, considering its condition."

Billy Lang had died so this Frenchy could brag glibly about buying back that cursed coat! Thomas let the trap slip from his grasp and coiled his fist.

"I know what you are thinking, Roebuck, but it will have to wait. I owe you satisfaction, and you shall have it. But now we must get out of here. We will go to the Huron camp. You will be safe."

"On the word of a liar and a thief?"

Etienne dropped his eyes. "On the holy mother of God," he said earnestly.

Before dusk fell, the men were seated on rush mats in the Huron hunting camp, their horses and mules secure, scooping fingersful of sagamité paste into their mouths and diluting the mealy blandness with a sour, fermented drink. Etienne was apparently well-known to these Hurons, for after being formally welcomed, his presence caused only passing interest.

A brave came to pause before them. He looked Thomas over and posed a question. Etienne threw back his head and laughed.

"He asks if you are my prisoner. He offers to buy you. They need a trade to the Iroquois for some of their own men." He waited, teeth gleaming in the black beard and moustache, watching Thomas with that sharp-eyed glance Thomas remembered.

He said indifferently, "You did not chase me across a wilderness to feed me to your friends."

"Perhaps you want to share your silver with me in gratitude, *mon ami*."

Thomas barked out a mirthless laugh. "For openers, Etienne Harmonie, if that is indeed who you are, I have no silver. The money from the furs I sold at Onondaga, is that what you speak of? It is the form of credits, long since sent to a friend for safe keeping. No man in his right mind travels with silver or gold; you should know that. And second, what makes you think I value my life so that I would care very much if you did deal me off to the Iroquois?" He leaned back on an elbow and stretched his muscular legs before him. His blue eyes had gone a flinty gray, challenging the Frenchman.

Etienne dropped the bantering guise. He sighed. "You are right. It was not for this that I bribed a minion of your General Roger Wolcott's staff to find you."

"You did what? *Why?*"

"A Harmonie pays his debts. . . . It was Christian charity that prompted me to send your coat to your father. I was with the—party—that ambushed your men. Not of my own free will! I came to the New World to escape the machinations of kings."

"Providence must play its little jokes," Thomas conceded bitterly.

"Ah, Roebuck, it is a joke, is it not? Bad blood between Louis and George and so France and England must war, and the devil be blamed."

"And you Papists get the Indians to do your dirty work."

"As you pagans have not?" Etienne rejoined sharply. He thrust out a booted leg and pulled up his trouser. The sallow skin of his calf was deeply ridged with long, parallel scars. "Your Iroquois brothers were turning me into a bloody work of art while the redcoats cheered them on."

Thomas looked away. It was easier to hate an enemy if you could convince yourself your friends were somehow nobler. "They traded you, finally?"

"Yes. Three English so-called fur traders for three of ours."

Thomas smiled grimly. "I do not see that you owe me a debt, Harmonie. And if you did, you have paid it today."

Etienne had told Thomas as they rode into the camp how his act of compassion had rebounded. When his letter to Thomas's father had eventually reached the Huguenot women, his aunt, Marie Therese, had written to him. His first reaction had been joy that she and Gennie were safe in the New World. But it was in this way that Etienne had eventually learned that he himself had set in motion the chain of events that led to the unhappy marriage of his cousin.

"That is why I had to seek you out," he said now. "I shall always regret causing my little cousin—and you, Roebuck—more pain, when she has had so much already."

Thomas's mind was in turmoil. A simple act of charity. How could a simple act of charity so completely wreck the lives of two people who loved each other? *Why?* Thomas shifted unhappily. His foot throbbed. He was not a man who liked to analyze things. He preferred to act. And he felt wretchedly uncomfortable having this proud coureur de bois humble himself. God help him, he liked the man!

"Tell me, Harmonie. Why did you steal my furs and not my pa's mule, back in forty-five?"

A look of surprise crossed Etienne's face, as if the question was not at all what he had been expecting. He grinned. "Simple. You were trapping the Alleghenies. That is my territory. Therefore the furs were mine by right. The mule was not mine."

Thomas had to laugh. Nothing had changed, but his mood felt suddenly lighter.

They remained in the Huron camp for two days, while Thomas's foot healed. The Hurons agreed to provide an escort that would take him to the edge of the Miamis' territory, from which point he would be safe.

During these days, Thomas plied Etienne with questions, filling his starved mind with details of Gennie's France.

"How is it that Gennie's branch of the family became Protestant and yours did not?"

Etienne shrugged eloquently. "I remember our fathers arguing about it. Gennie was too young to understand. She was only nine when I left. For me, leaving was easier than examining my own faith. She and I never talked about our parents' differences when we were together. It was enough to feel God's loving presence."

He paused and added thoughtfully, "My father was horrified when Uncle Flourinot was murdered. He knew Huguenots had been persecuted in the past. But he thought that was behind us. France is too great a land for that . . ."

Finally, Thomas brought himself to say, "From your letters from Madame Harmonie, how is Gennie now?" Did he hope that she was happy? Had she forgotten him?

Etienne stared away morosely. "She—they—have a baby. A son."

Irrational anger rose like gorge in Thomas's throat. That should have been his baby! The devil take them both.

Etienne wisely left him alone for the next hour as they continued riding side by side in the direction of La Demoiselle's camp.

The braves indicated they had reached the border. They prepared to turn back. Etienne interpreted for Thomas. Roebuck leaned over his horse to extend his hand to the man who had befriended him.

"Thank you, Harmonie. When all this is over, we may meet

again." But would he want to meet again? with the painful reminder of all he had lost?

Etienne smiled. "Peace and happiness, Thomas Roebuck."

"And to you—Etienne. Godspeed."

The men clasped hands again. Thomas watched as Etienne wheeled his horse and trotted northward after the Hurons. He would miss the Frenchman. At the same time Thomas was relieved. He had feared for a time that Etienne planned to accompany him all the way. It would not do for the French to get wind of the dispatches he carried, nor of the concessions Wolcott wanted him to win for the Americans.

La Demoiselle was a wily and experienced statesman. Certainly capable of playing off his favors between French and English as they crossed his lands.

icking his way down the wooded hills sloping toward the upper Miami River, Thomas paused, well concealed amid leafy bowers, to observe a band of men far below. He caught glints of a river and the sun striking a standard from which fluttered a pennant. Uniforms, Black Robes, Indians, and woodsmen. A large company. They appeared to have stopped only briefly to bury something. The party remounted and disappeared southward in orderly fashion.

Thomas triangulated the spot mentally and proceeded down the hillside. What the French had partially buried was a metal survey plate, claiming the land on both sides of the river as the personal domain of King Louis of France. Thomas snorted in surprise. To his knowledge, this land was claimed by Pennsylvania, that not in Indian territory.

He dug up the heavy marker and secured it in the mule's pack. He reckoned he was only two day's ride from the camp of La Demoiselle. Could the group he had just seen be heading there also, in another effort to persuade the chief to cast his lot with the French? If they could woo him, all the Miamis would follow.

He recalled what he knew of La Demoiselle. The English called him Old Britain for his steadfast loyalty. He had been known to sit through hours of ceremonious meetings as French priests and citizen-soldiers urged him to relocate his camp on the Maumee, near a French post there, where his tribe "could be protected from the English."

La Demoiselle had listened, accepted their gifts, and said, "Not now." Instead, after the French had left, La Demoiselle had issued a call to his people, had built an enormous fortified warehouse to house the furs his hunters harvested, and located his people's tepees around his own "fort."

This was before Thomas had met him. That visionary thinking had only increased Thomas's respect for the man. Too often people fought new ways, even when they were good ways. By entering into fur trading in the white man's fashion, La Demoiselle was seeking to ensure his people's share of the future. His reputation for fearless integrity, his skills as a leader, had already brought many English families to dwell among the Miamis at his generous invitation.

As he neared Pickawillany, La Demoiselle's domain, the land

stretched out before Thomas in fine, level pasture, and well-timbered forests of ash, walnut, cherry, and sugar trees. Well-watered meadows abounded in wild rye, bluegrass and clover. He heard singing bees, and the raucous call of turkeys, watched leisurely herds of deer and elk. Once he spotted a herd of thirty or forty of the great beasts he'd heard called buffalo.

What a place to build a home, to raise crops and—yes, raise a family. He was twenty now, time to think of settling down. Gennie might be lost to him, but he could still become a good husband and father. When he had lost her, God had directed him into the path chosen by General Wolcott. It had been a good decision, Thomas reflected, gazing about him.

The explosion of ripe color and fulsome sound exalted his spirits. Small wonder that Indians, in their struggle to account for the creation of such a bounteous land, had invested a myriad of nature gods. Drinking in the abundance, Thomas felt reconciled. Here, in this land, there was a chance for him to find peace. And perhaps Providence would direct him to a godly woman to share his life.

In the distance he sighted a large log structure that could easily be mistaken for one belonging to the white race. Nearly as well fortified as Le Detroit, it sat in the midst of a flat, ancient plain. Among the meandering streams of the plain clustered painted tepees and some permanent log cabins.

He remembered the shock he felt the first time he visited La Demoiselle's camp, to see a squaw with her nose cut off. La Demoiselle had shrugged and informed him that she had spent too much time preening while other women were working in the cornfields!

It was a village larger than Germantown, a gathering of some six hundred fires scattered around the warehouse. Friendly children and dogs raced up to greet him, and squaws nodded shyly from their work. He'd never seen more industrious women, kneeling among knee-high stands of corn, working among beans, pumpkins, and squash vines.

He passed gatherings of braves talking here and there, just as similar groups might linger before a tavern. He noticed that none of the men seemed to be engaged in fruitful labor. Only the women, in all the tribes he had visited, did manual labor. By the braves' reasoning, they hunted and fished and sat on councils, and which, after all, was more important?

As he neared the warehouse, Thomas noticed with chagrin the string of horses and pack mules of the party of Frenchmen he had spotted two days ago. No wonder Etienne had not insisted on riding all the way with him! He probably knew that French interests were already being looked after.

The chief and his guests were seated in the open on mats before enormous piles of furs. Well, he had interrupted a trading session.

La Demoiselle presented a magnificent figure at perhaps forty-five years, clad in a breechclout and wearing copper ornaments in his ears. His iron gray hair was plaited in two braids and slicked with bear grease, which also gleamed on his arms and chest. His muscles rippled under the firm, copper skin as he rose to greet Thomas as he dismounted.

His guests also rose as a matter of courtesy.

"Céleron de Bienville, emissary of his majesty, King Louis," a confident-looking man garbed like any trapper introduced himself. He turned to his left. "Brother Julliard and Brother Auguste." The two Black Robes nodded with just the correct amount of restraint. The Indians accompanying them were Ottawas, from the region of Pontchartrain.

Thomas acknowledged the introductions. He had strong feelings he was witnessing an accelerated flanking movement by the French, part of their unrelenting attempt to isolate the English along the coast. For the French to entice La Demoiselle away from his English leanings would be a major setback in the struggle to keep France and Spain from locking the new American colonies in, shutting them out of the explorations of the western frontiers.

In a ceremonial pile, on a separate mat, Thomas noted flasks he presumed contained brandy and pouches that might have held the wonderful French tobacco, both dear to Indians.

Half a century ago, French priests had succeeded in making it a criminal act to give strong spirits to Indians, having seen its effect upon them and compassionately desiring to protect them. Over the years, however, seeing the English benefiting as Indians brought them furs for whiskey, when the French refused them brandy, the French had relented to the realities of trade and begun once again to offer brandy in exchange for prime furs.

"Less than a moon's walk," La Demoiselle was saying, his arm extended southward, "are other men who pray using beads like yours."

De Bienville exchanged glances with the priests. "Our Spanish brothers," said Brother Julliard.

De Bienville posed an urgent question to La Demoiselle in French.

La Demoiselle smiled and answered in English, "We have made

long talks. I will now see to my new guest; then we will meet to eat."

He nodded at Thomas, which Thomas took to mean he should follow, and rose gracefully to his feet. La Demoiselle possessed enormous dignity. His eyes were the same iron gray as his hair. He had a way of gazing at petitioners as if seeing beyond their faces, into their thoughts.

As they strolled leisurely around the busy village he said, "I am pleased to see you have decided not to die after all."

Thomas threw him a startled glance.

La Demoiselle smiled. "Last year death was your friend. He is no longer with you."

Thomas was stuck for an answer, so the chief went on, "Have you taken a wife yet, Roebuck?"

"No, sir."

La Demoiselle nodded. By design or coincidence they came to stop at a compound that was a hive of activity. Some women were plaiting fresh sleeping mats or weaving baskets. Others cleaned fish and strung them to dry over low fires. A third group was scraping animal skins stretched on frames, while half-grown girls tended children too small to be left unwatched.

"It is time you did."

"Soon, perhaps. If Providence wills."

La Demoiselle let the matter rest.

As they walked on, Thomas looked up at the chief, who was nearly a head taller than he. "I also brought gifts for you, from the great English king." On an impulse he added, "And also something to show you that is not a gift but a warning."

La Demoiselle continued his stately pace. "Warnings are as plentiful as fleas." As if to point this up, he scratched his head, located a flea with a forefinger, and extricated it. He scrutinized it, then ate it.

Thomas stared, astonished. This from La Demoiselle was as unthinkable as it would have been from General Wolcott!

La Demoiselle smiled. "It is not that they taste good. It is to get even."

Thomas threw back his head and laughed. He was just beginning to appreciate this Miami's sense of humor.

They reached the tepee that Thomas was to use. Moments later, inside, he showed the chief the survey plate. "It is a way men have of establishing boundaries."

"Like an animal lifting a leg."

"Something like that. This means that despite what the Frenchman says to you, in his mind he already possesses your land."

La Demoiselle grunted scornfully. "This does not surprise me. Come." And a few minutes later, "There, you see?" He pointed out a French flag. "I did not invite them to plant their flag inside my village. I accept their gifts, and I tell them no . . ." His fingers caressed the smooth jaw line thoughtfully. Suddenly he said, "A courier has left a message for you, entrusted to my care." Said proudly—a man who was taken into confidences knew his friends.

In the privacy of his tepee, Thomas unwrapped the leather pouch La Demoiselle had given him. He withdrew a heavy parchment scroll sealed with a glob of blue wax imprinted with General Wolcott's seal. The message was terse, without salutation or signature.

A private company calling itself the Ohio Company of Virginia has made claim to 500,000 thousand acres between where this missive finds you and Penn's colony. This could end all peaceful coexistence with tribes of that area, including your host.

Whether the so-called Ohio Company can muster the manpower and the legislative backing to enforce their claims may well depend upon the willingness of all colonial assemblies to honor our previous treaties with the Indian nations. I tell you this: The French are not the worst of our enemies. Private greed and public chicanery are with us forever. . . .

Thomas could never remember Wolcott so pessimistic. He read the final paragraph: "Incidentally, King George's good counselors have persuaded the Crown to return Fort Louisbourg to the French. Our command must be relinquished by next summer."

Thomas let out an oath and crushed the parchment in his fist. Why? Why? A blithe act of politics, robbing the war of reason, erasing meaning from hundreds of dead. And for what?

He lowered himself to the ground, sitting cross-legged, his elbows propped on his knees, his fingers clutching the parchment. For what good? Higgins—other men of his battery who had died or been maimed, those killed in ambush with Billy Lang. *Any* good from it? His friendship with Peter Sparhawk, which he knew would continue, though the men saw each other rarely now. His respect and admiration for Roger Wolcott. Those were good.

But balanced against this, the shock and disruption of lives. His own family, abandoning their farm for a time to move in with relatives in Harper's Ferry and only recently returning to Germantown. And Gennie, his precious Gennie . . .

What must he do? La Demoiselle was a man of honor. He governed well the vast numbers of Indians and others in his territory. Thomas's original brief contained treaties for the extension of fur trapping and trading privileges by men of all the English colonies.

The Ohio Company presumably meant to challenge the French fur-trading route of the Saint Lawrence seaway and the English Mohawk Valley route as well; they would establish an alternate route farther south, one with better weather, one that led to the interior by a way through the mountains and from the sea. It wasn't enough to share the limitless wealth of this golden land: They wanted a monopoly, 500,000 acres to themselves.

To deny the French claim was one thing. To deny Pennsylvania's claim and treaties already in existence between the tribes and various other colonies was blatant greed and a bid for power.

Being a man of no political ambitions, Thomas began to feel disgust for all such manipulations. Perhaps there was even somewhere a secret treaty between France and England, using the New World as their chessboard: You give us back Louisbourg, and we will not fuss over your land grab.

If the Ohio Company did succeed in grinding out of existence all other claims in the area, how long would they hold their monopoly? Only until someone else came along with bolder dreams and a bigger appetite.

How could he help La Demoiselle and his people? Warnings are like fleas, he had said. They did not alter the course of destiny. Perhaps not. But still one could be prepared.

———————— ◆ ————————

"My counsel to you." Thomas sat cross-legged in a circle in the council tent, ringed by La Demoiselle and his advisors. "Sign no more treaties. Maintain lines of friendship with all, but trust none. Be prepared to fight for your tribal lands even as you continue to be honorable in your dealings with all, as God would have us all do."

La Demoiselle leaned forward, his gray eyes shadowed, his face immobile.

Does he believe me? "I have learned by sad experience that both my brothers the English and the French will use your tribe as they have used others—to continue the war against each other. To our own ends we inflame tribe against tribe, use renegade braves to stir trouble. You must be wary and beware of all who come bearing gifts and papers to sign."

Saying these words, Thomas felt a hundred years old. Yet he knew of no other way to help this peaceful tribe survive amidst two giants to whom peaceful coexistence was never a reality, but always a temporary expedient.

"I shall leave you at dawn tomorrow, Chief La Demoiselle." He stood in the refreshing twilight after the council meeting had ended, tamping his pipe with French tobacco just offered by the chief, flanked by him and two of his sons.

"You have been honest with us in a way no other has been," said La Demoiselle. "Now it is my wish that you accept lands, as much as you can walk in a day and a half, and dwell among us. It is also my wish for you to take a wife."

A lump of gratitude formed in Thomas's throat. He clasped La Demoiselle's hand with great feeling. "I will be proud to dwell with you. I have no wish to live among the sad memories of my own people."

La Demoiselle took a few thoughtful paces. "I have also decided to sign the treaties you brought, in spite of your words. I have told the French fathers we have made a road to the sunrising and have been taken by the hand by our brothers the English, the Six Nations, the Delawares, Shawnees, and the Wyandots. In that road we will go, and as the fathers have threatened us with a war in the spring, we tell you we are ready to receive them."

"I will relay your message faithfully," promised Thomas. "We are honored that you remain our friend." Thomas gazed out over the shadowed silhouettes of distant hills. "The land you have chosen is beautiful beyond compare."

La Demoiselle smiled. "I myself chose this site." He and his sons walked away.

In a moment, Father Auguste stepped out of the shadows. "I would that I had been privileged to hear your counsel, English."

Thomas glanced around swiftly at his voice. How much had he heard?

"Shall we walk?" His English was near perfect. Leisurely he stepped out on the path taken by the chief and his sons, his sturdy sandals slapping softly against the earth. "If the savages could learn to love God as easily as they learn to fear the French, Christianity would conquer the land."

"Christianity will conquer the land," Thomas stared levelly at the Black Robe, "but not with the aid of men who consider their brothers savages. I find their suspicion of your religion not so different from your attitude toward Protestants." *Might not this Black Robe be the very one who cast Gennie's father and brother to their deaths in Le Havre?*

"There is all the difference in the world between passing into hell and passing into the Living World of our Savior."

"Providence is cruel," replied Thomas, "but not so cruel as to deny all but Catholics eternal rest in him."

The Black Robe studied him in silence. "So much bitterness, my son? Is there something you wish to talk about?" His voice had altered subtly and now seemed filled with compassion.

For a moment Thomas was tempted to pour out his own soul, his disillusionment, his sorrow. He turned his head and cursed himself for weakness.

"Then, tell me something." The priest's voice was once again businesslike.

"If I am able."

"Why does La Demoiselle hate us? The French have never harmed him or his people."

"I have been told he is a very wise man. Perhaps he does not believe it would be good for his people to adopt the Catholic faith."

"Careful, young man! You are beginning to sound like a heretic yourself."

"Providence has not always treated me well, priest. Yet my trust remains in God. And I believe that through his Son there are many paths to Glory." He strode away into the darkness.

Thomas left camp at dawn, with firm assurances to La Demoiselle that he would return one day, to stay, if Providence willed.

La Demoiselle smiled into his eyes. "The Great Spirit is in you. You will be back—do you know White Woman's Creek?"

"No."

"It lies within the way of your return home. It is named for the woman living there now."

"A white woman?"

"Yes. Here she is know as Woman-Who-Hides. Her English name is Mary Harris. She was brought to my village years ago and given to one of my braves in marriage. He was killed in a war, and she chose not to have another husband, as was her right. I gave permission for her to live apart with her children. I would count it a favor if you would visit her and remind her that her people still think of her. See that her wants are met, and I will count it a second favor."

"I will do as you ask." Thomas listened intently as La Demoiselle recounted the streams and paths he must follow, the landmarks to seek, in order to find Mary Harris of White Woman's Creek.

Last he pressed into Thomas's hand a calumet. It was as long as his arm, hewed of red stone, hollowed, painted, and carved. The pipe would allow him to pass through even hostile tribes' territories unmolested. His hand closed around the pipe, and he thanked La Demoiselle from his heart.

There was a special magic to the new day as he rode out of the camp. The spun gold of dawn paled into the heat of midday. All nature grew pensive as though suspended in timeless moments. Overhead not a glossy leaf stirred. Horse and mule padded on, on a welcome thick carpet of mold matter. That day and the next and the next Thomas grew gradually absorbed in the life around him, as though he, too, were part of the special transformation of season. The breathless waiting, the heat-shimmery promise of golden days yet coming before winter, the inertia of living in the bosom of a beneficent Mother.

One day he heard a woman's voice singing, a deep and hearty song. Snatches of it sounded like Indian chanting, but here and there a phrase of a hymn slipped out. He had been following White Woman's Creek a day and a half. This late in summer it was reduced to a mere trickle, easy to follow since a well-worn path ran beside it.

Through leafy trees he saw glimpses of dead white and tried to imagine what it might be. Soon he entered a patch of garden. As he drew up he realized the white was a washing, such as his mother might have done, that was spread on rocks and hanging from brittle boughs to dry. He grinned. Folks were sure more alike than different.

"Mary Harris!" he bellowed at the cabin.

He heard a cry of exclamation. A young woman rushed to the door. He caught a blur of long, chestnut hair, a mouth open in soundless shock in a white face. Her small fists clenched and her elbows retreated into her sides before she slipped into a dead faint.

Thomas reared in the stirrups. "Gennie!"

homas leaped from his horse. He reached the crumpled form of the girl just as a massive woman appeared behind her in the doorway.

"What happened to my girl?" she bellowed.

Tenderly Thomas cradled Gennie's head and shoulders. Her thick hair tumbled over his arms.

"Gennie." His voice shook. The color began to come back into her face. Her skin held a soft tan glow. Gone was the roundness of her cheeks, that had bloomed so rosily against her fine skin. Her heart-shaped face appeared more angular. Only her full lips, raspberry hued and sweetly parted, seemed unchanged.

Thomas felt overwhelmed with love. He longed to crush her fragile body to him, to taste her sweet lips again, and feel her cool arms twine behind his neck. He was astounded at the sudden strength of the passion that seized him, which he had thought was dead. He knew now that he would never get over his love for Gennie.

When he could control his voice, he said, "What is wrong with her? How did she get here?"

"Who are you?" the woman boomed back.

Thomas looked up. "You are Mary Harris, aren't you? How did Gennie get here?"

Mary Harris was dressed as the Miami women had been, though her buckskin shift had no beaded or painted decoration. Below the knee-length fringe, a bright calico skirt fell to her ankles. Her feet were sandaled. But it was her face, framed in a rich mass of gray hair, that arrested him. She had wide, parched-looking lips and stern, smoky eyes under thick brows. A strong face. He could understand a woman like this calmly telling a chief that she would prefer to live alone in the woods.

Mary Harris repeated her question. "Who are *you*, and how did you get here? Gennie, is it? That her name? I warrant she's all right; you gave her a shock."

Gennie's eyes fluttered open. She gazed at Thomas with a mystified expression. Her eyes traveled to Mary. Instantly she held out her arms to the woman, to be helped up. Instinctively Thomas released his grasp as Mary helped her to her feet.

"Bless you, child, it is someone you know, isn't it?" A muscular arm protectively about Gennie, Mary Harris said, "I do not know who you are, but if you know this poor girl, then 'twas a special Providence that sent you."

Gennie gazed at him with somber curiosity.

"She doesn't act afraid of you, that's to the good . . . Gennie? Tell Mary you are Gennie."

Gennie's lips slowly and gently pressed together.

Mary *tched* and shook her head. She hugged Gennie and then released her. Moving like an obedient child, Gennie headed for the cabin. Thomas took a step after her, and Mary threw up a warning hand. As Gennie disappeared inside, Mary gave Thomas a crooked smile.

"For all I know, you are the one caused her to be like this."

Thomas started to protest. Mary shrugged. "Didn't say you was."

"I am here because of La Demoiselle. As a favor. To look in on you. Permit me, madam. Thomas Roebuck, of Germantown, Pennsylvania. Please, for the love of God, tell me about Gennie!"

"Unhitch your animals, Thomas Roebuck. If you can bide a day or two, we might make some sense o' this." Mary seated herself comfortably on a log that had been axed into a short bench with a right-angled back rest and pulled a pipe out of a pouch slung over her shift.

Thomas glanced toward the cabin.

"Go on, look. I can tell you what she'll be doing. She has her own little corner."

His heart beat fearfully. O God, what was the matter with her? What had happened? He stepped softly inside. Immediately he sensed a peaceful feeling. There was the aroma of a meat stew simmering over a hearth fire. The cabin had small windows cut in three sides, admitting some light. On all sides, the pegged walls held clothing and supplies in drawstring bags. A table and benches made of split planks occupied the center of the room. Placed against the walls were four pallets, raised off the floor by wood frames. On one of these sat his Gennie.

Her feet tucked up beneath her skirts, Gennie sat with both arms clasped around a smallish, leather-bound book. Her brown eyes dominated her face, following him as he came closer.

"Gennie?" he whispered. He stopped about four paces away. "Gennie, it's Thomas. You know me. I'm Thomas." His voice broke. He could see she didn't know him. "You do know me. I would not hurt you for the world." Tears spilled freely down his cheeks. "Oh, Gennie . . ." He reached a hand toward her and she nestled against the wall, away from him.

"Gennie, . . . I'm not ever going to leave you again. I don't know what happened, but I vow before God that I won't leave you, and I won't let anything happen to you as long as I live."

She looked friendly and withdrawn at the same time. Suddenly she bent her head and seemed totally absorbed in the book on her lap.

Thomas straightened. He brushed his eyes with the back of his sleeve and waited until he had hold again. Then he retreated into the brightness of the day.

Mary squinted through the smoke of her pipe and waited.

"She come late spring," she began finally. "Carrying a dead baby boy in her arms. Two days before she'd give up the poor critter. Wouldn't let my sons touch her, but she didn't act afraid of me. My sons speak only the Miami tongue." Mary explored the inside of her cheek with her tongue, ruminatively. "At first she didn't act too bad off. She even spoke first day or so. Well, wasn't English. French, I think. Seemed to understand English, though. When I finally got her to give up the baby, that's when she stopped talking at all. When she understood it was dead. Shall I show you where we buried it?"

Thomas could stand it no longer. The big, kindly woman looked away as his body shook with sobs. He threw a forearm across his face and stumbled into the woods. "I'll make them pay!" He pounded a futile fist against a tree. "I will make them pay!"

When he could, he returned to the clearing. Mary paid no attention. She knocked her pipe against the bench, to remove the ashes, and said, "Come. It is better to get it over with."

She moved with feline grace through a copse of trees surrounding a natural bower. Here was a tiny, tended grave, strewn with fresh wild flowers.

"Spirit-Who-Cries—Gennie she is to you—spends many hours here."

Upon the grave rested an animal skull. Thomas threw Mary a quizzical expression.

"When a little child dies, my husband's people cut off the head of a dog and place it upon the grave. Dogs can always find their way. Even when he is frightened, the child willingly goes with the dog through the spirit world, and it guides the child to the human spirits." Her quiet voice died away, and they listened to the wind.

A deep sigh swept through him.

"Are you the baby's father?"

"It should have been so." Haltingly he told her the short tale of their courtship and her marriage to another.

"Then she is wed."

With a shock Thomas realized this was true. And by all that was holy, he was bound to restore her to her husband. Never! He had promised never to let her go, and he would not. They would return to the Miamis. He could not take her home! Since they had not found Gennie by this time, they would believe her dead.

But while one side of him argued thus, the other taunted that he could not marry her, could never live with her as husband to wife in the blessed sight of God.

"She had no marriage ring," Mary was saying. "I thought the child the reason she was driven out. That would be like the English."

Thomas looked at her in surprise. "Is that what happened to you?" It slipped out before he realized the utter rudeness of such a question. Thomas stumbled all over himself apologizing.

Mary just looked as if she had not really expected better. "I was born in the province of Massachusetts. I was seven years old when I was stolen from my family. Later I was sold to the Miamis. It was many summers before the English explorers came this far west. By then I was a young wife. I loved my husband. The language came back to me, little by little, as trappers came by. I would translate for La Demoiselle. All that was long ago. Now, of course, he speaks English. I have seen the English come and treat us like animals. Marrying my sisters, then leaving them with no one to protect them, no one to furnish meat for their families."

"La Demoiselle said your husband is dead now."

"Long time." Woman-Who-Hides smiled and started back toward the cabin, Thomas following. "I could have accepted another husband, good strong woman that I am, without a reputation for quarrelsomeness. La Demoiselle even offered to send me back to my first people." Thomas heard her snort. "I had no desire to go, so I asked his permission to live alone. I am a fair shot, and my boys are nearly grown—they are away on a hunting trip now—we live well here."

"La Demoiselle sent you some rice from the swamps," Thomas said absently. "He says you are partial to it." They had reached the cabin, and he turned to stare back into the woods from which they had come.

"I shall take Gennie with me." He swung his gaze to Mary, as if challenging her to deny his right.

"She may not want to go. In that case she will escape at the first chance. Wait a quarter of the moon. Let her become used to you."

Thomas could see the wisdom in her words.

In the week that followed, he attempted to draw Gennie into conversation. She resisted. Finally he was forced to admit the possibility that she would not go with him. On the day before he was to leave, he said to her, "Gennie, I must leave tomorrow. I am carrying dispatches that must be delivered. Do you hear, dear one? I want you to come with me. Gennie?" He tried to take her hand, but she drew it behind her back, lowering her lashes.

"Gennie, will you not talk to me? or nod, if you do not feel like talking yet? Gennie?" He tried to draw her face toward him as Mary had done, but at the touch of his finger under her chin she slipped away like quicksilver.

He hesitated, then followed her. She went directly to the little bower sheltering the baby's grave. Thomas waited, watching. Slowly Gennie sank to her knees and clasped her hands. Her lips moved. Her tears watered the grave. Silently he backed away.

Mary Harris came upon him an hour later, sitting in the clearing before the cabin.

"I do not know what to do," he confessed. "If she will not go with me tomorrow, my only decision will be whether to tell anyone I have found her. If she agrees to come, I am bound to return her to whatever horror she was escaping from . . .

"Yet, for all that I know, a grieving and loving husband is praying for her return. If that be so, then Providence is using me to fulfil another's destiny, and I dare not shirk my duty." Thomas buried his face in his hands.

"Humph." Mary Harris folded her burly arms. "If it were me, I would take her west and never look back."

Thomas spent most of the night on his knees, just as he had done over two years ago. Again, as then, his agony was caused by the young woman he knew belonged to him and no other. Did he, dare he, trust God enough to be obedient?

At dawn he packed the mule. Gennie watched his every move, as he and Mary observed hers. Finally he had no reason to delay longer. He turned to the women with a small gesture of helplessness.

Mary saw it. "Thank you for the furs. And the tobacco and rice. You are welcome here whenever you come this way again."

Gennie walked to Mary and took her arm.

Mary disengaged her hands and held them in hers. "Go with Thomas Roebuck, Gennie. Go, and get well."

Gennie's brow puckered. She pulled away and turned toward the cabin.

"Gennie!" Thomas's voice rang with anguish.

She did not stop.

"Mary . . ."

Mary shook her head. "Maybe next time, Thomas. Maybe her time of healing is not yet."

Suddenly Gennie reappeared. In her arms she carried her baby's bundled clothing, her journal, and balanced carefully on top, a dainty porcelain teacup and saucer, painted with daffodils.

Thomas took one look and shouted, "She knows me, Mary! She's coming!"

Gennie stopped to place her things on the ground and went to Mary. She cupped the woman's face in her hands, then embraced her. Her eyes were liquid with tears. Her face contorted with words that would not come.

"Yes, honey, Mary knows. She is coming with you, Thomas."

ith grim face Thomas headed east, back toward Germantown. Years later, he would remember this trek as his most agonizing test of faith. He had repacked the animals, splitting the load of supplies between horse and mule so that Gennie could ride the mule and be free to follow at her own pace.

At nightly campfires, he gave her all the separateness she seemed to need. He built the fires and prepared their meals. He hunted and fished. Occasionally Gennie smiled as he would return holding aloft a string of fat trout for their supper. It was hell, and it was heaven.

Just having Gennie here, beside him, feeling that she was at peace, was enough. But when she lay curled in furs, lost in sleep, and he watched the flicker of shadows and firelight across her fine features and in the tumble of her hair, then the tortures would rise in him again, and he would wrestle like Job with the problems of evil and obedience.

How could it be wrong to love a woman and want to take care of her and protect her? Had she left her husband, or had he cast her out? He thought of the Gennie that was buried inside the sleeping woman. Could she see him? Did she know that he was there, for her, when she was ready to face whatever horrors had driven her inside? And what if cruel fates were playing with him, and he was a puppet on the devil's string, returning Gennie to the evil that had created the horror?

———————•◆•———————

"So ye had to bring her here." William Roebuck leaned on the handle of his axe. Splits of cordwood lay about him. His face looked as obstinate as ever.

Thomas had hoped that the years' absence would have brought him and his father closer in understanding, as men.

"Always was stubborn. Once ye got it in your head ye had to have that French piece, wasn't no turnin' ye."

Thomas felt the old anger churning up. He bit back a sharp retort.

Not even his father's meanness of spirit could quench his happiness. Gennie was no longer married! The first thing he had learned yesterday, when he had brought her out of the forest to his parents' farm, was that Goodman Amos was dead and unlamented.

His mother had been ecstatic to see them. To Thomas's immense gratitude, she had made Gennie welcome and smothered her with warmth and understanding. Let his pa wrap his tight-faced disapproval about himself like a shroud. Thomas no longer cared.

William Roebuck was watching him, resting on the axe. "There's talk she's devil teched," he needled. "Who knows what them Indians did to her?" He heaved the axe above his shoulder and swung downward with a powerful blow, shattering the wood and causing pieces of kindling to fly in the air. The axe head drove deep in the stump.

Thomas braced his legs apart and fortified himself against giving in to his own anger. "It is what God-fearing, civilized folk did to her, Pa."

"She left here with a baby. Shamed her husband into an early grave, and now you brought her back and tell me she kilt her baby too."

"Not what I said, Pa."

" 'Tis what people will think."

"No, I do not care what people think! I brought her back because it was the only right thing to do. I'm no hypocrite: I am thankful her husband is dead, because now she is free to marry me. And just as soon as we can, I am taking her out west, to the Ohio valley. I got my own land out there, Pa." *Land. My own land.* He could hardly wait to get back!

For the first time, William met his eyes. "She's teched, son," he wheedled helplessly. "Any fool kin see that. You gonna marry a teched woman?"

"God led me to find her, and now he's made it so I can take care of her proper." It was Thomas's turn to stare obstinately ahead. "It is going to be all right, I know it."

"Uh-huh. You going to marry a crazy woman and go back and live with the Indians."

Roebuck resumed chopping with a vengeance, shutting him out, unwilling even to listen to him.

Thomas wheeled and strode back to the house. The key, it seemed to him, must rest in the diary or journal that Gennie never let out of her sight. Without knowing what it contained, he might never learn what drove Gennie from her home. That night, while Gennie slept, his mother slipped it out from her bedclothes.

"What are you going to do with it, Thomas?"

"Ride into town. I intend to ask Gennie's mother to translate it."

His mother was silent a moment. "Did you know that Marie Therese married Henri Zellaire?"

"No."

She shrugged. "Well, they *are* married."

Thomas picked up the diary his mother had laid beside the tallow candle. Reverently he opened the soft leather cover. On the first page he read, "Genevieve Harmonie, ma livre, Septiembre, 1744." His hand closed around the book. The secrets of a girl's insanity. And the key, if Providence willed, to her recovery.

Marie Therese closed her daughter's diary. Pushing it away, she laid her arms on the table, lowered her head, and moaned, *"Mon Dieu, mon Dieu,* I knew it. I am her mother. I should have done something."

Thomas stared down at her, his eyes slitted with loathing for the dead man. His big knuckles whitened around the condemning journal.

"I do not understand you, Madame Harmonie—Madame Zellaire."

Her words came up muffled, her head still buried in her arms. "You are wondering . . . how I could marry a man who . . . who indirectly caused my daughter so much suffering. Gennie was right, in her diary. Goodman Amos did trade her for two slaves who would be more useful to Henri than she was. Henri was an instrument of his own greed."

The head of rich, chestnut hair, so like Gennie's, raised. Marie Therese sat very erect. Her reddened eyes sent a stern glance at Thomas. "But he was also a generous man to send the money for our escape from France in the first place. Forgiveness is better than bitterness. I know. God brings each of us to crossroads, not once, but many times. I could have spent my life within convent walls, gradually earning my peace and dissolving my unhappiness in acceptance of his will. But another door opened. I am not sorry that Gennie and I took that door."

"But letting Gennie marry that old man!"

Marie Therese was silent. Then she said quietly, "Do you understand, Thomas? An indentured foreigner, with no dowry, no family, no one to vouch that she is a person of value, does not have many choices. Other marriages such as the one Gennie made have been richly blessed. That Gennie's was not does not change that."

An involuntary shudder went through his frame. "It sounds so cold-blooded."

"And you sound as if you forget that our blessed Savior is still in charge." Briefly, a smile touched her face. "He has imperfect material through which to work his will. He whom you call Providence. Then it was Providence that sent you to the camp of the savage—no? Who sent you on to rescue Gennie?"

Thomas paced moodily around the comfortable room. His fingers traced the top of the silent spinning wheel, where he had first glimpsed Gennie.

"Who is this woman you read about in Gennie's diary, the 'only one who can help'?"

"I am not sure," said her mother. "Gennie's husband kept her away from me. The servants could tell you, her servants possibly. Or ...," Marie Therese put her finger to her lips, "there is one other. I saw them speaking together a few times at the mercantile ..."

<hr />

The next day Thomas found Rosalind Hambleton working in her vegetable garden. Her skirts were tucked up in the waistband of her maroon calico. Perspiration shone on her dark face, under the dappled shade of her straw hat.

Rosalind, still shaking her head and smiling over the good news that Gennie was alive, finally said, "Yes, I was the one. She didn't have no one else. Sometimes people gotta help people simply 'caise ain't no one else around.

"She come here with that po li'l chile, an' I like to die with pity. Should 'a seen 'em, Mistah Roebuck. She never was no bigger than a minute, an that baby was some sight. I knew when I delivered it, it wasn't right. You could see right off. Mouth all hangin' funny ... And that one eye red! Well, the night we came here after he was baptised, I tried to take it, so she could rest a bit, but she held on to it something fierce, even when she's sleepin'. Was all I could do to get her to take some supper. See, she's so 'fraid Mistah Amos find out where she's at and make trouble. Lordy you shoulda seen the bruises. Even when she was yellin' in labor she had bruises where she shouldn't of. I told her ain't nobody should put up with that, 'specially she bein' his wife an all, but she says who's to stop it? I ax her her momma know, and she says Mistah Amos never left them alone so's she could tell. An that poor chile! . . . I sure never figured he'd do her so bad."

Thomas turned his back to Rosalind. His voice shook with anguish, "What kind of God lets people be treated like that?"

"Same God as 'lowed Moses to have slaves, I 'spect," said Rosalind.

homas wiped the sweat from his brow. In the distance he could see Henri Zellaire's boy, Jean, now ten, balancing on one leg on a tree stump, his arms outstretched like a scarecrow, the other leg wavering askew.

"Cock-a-doodle-doo," he sang, jumping agilely down and flapping after a chicken that had strayed into the vegetable garden. The hen was one of a dozen that pecked and clucked in the dooryard of the new, thatch-roofed cabin.

Thomas had to smile. It was himself he was seeing as a youngster, playing when he could escape the chores his father always found with such vengeance, wondering how his father could stand to plod back and forth in a field all day, behind an unimaginative mule, when there were so many more exciting things to do.

But his father had never lost the half-angry tone he used with him as a boy. Never agreed that fishing and trapping were mighty fine, only that growing crops was necessary.

How to explain, then, his own aching joy at wrestling behind his own plow, on the land La Demoiselle had given him, the deed recorded on a wampum?

He heard Rosalind Hambleton's voice calling. The boy's red head went up, then he changed direction and disappeared down a bank tasseled with trees. Within minutes Jean reappeared, lugging one end of a wicker basket. On the other end was Rosalind, her skirts hiked to the boot tops and tucked in her waistband. Between them they hauled the heavy basket to a line of corded rope stretched between two poles. Rosalind began draping and smoothing wet bed linens over the line, and the boy took off again.

Was that a movement in the doorway? No.

The sorrow was fuller this morning. Perhaps because of his own remembered boyhood, his certainty then that there was nothing wrong with the world that wouldn't some day come out right. If you were good, you were rewarded. A benign Providence shone over all the earth and the good folk in it.

Thomas bent his broad shoulders to search among the lower leaves of the cornstalks. He had sown it as La Demoiselle's women had shown him, with bean vines planted to grow up the stalks. The corn was ripening nicely. They had had a few ears to eat already.

Plenty more coming along. And a full harvest to dry for winter, he'd be bound. Now and again he pulled off a ripe ear and lobbed it into a basket a few yards away, at the end of the row.

"Yep, Lord," he said to God, continuing a conversation begun earlier this morning. "You gave me what I asked for. I'd be less a man if I complained. I guess, Lord, when I asked you to trust me with Gennie, I didn't know how much caring that would be."

His blue eyes deepened a shade as he glanced again toward the cabin. He heard a robin sing and shook his head with a smile. Gennie had been with him two months now, over the tearful protests of Marie Therese, but with Henri's relieved blessing. Little Jean had been allowed to come, too. He and Gennie had always had a special bond of affection, and Thomas thought one could do worse than have a noisy lad about to stir things up.

During the harsh months of winter in Germantown, Marie Therese had tried everything she knew to restore Gennie's mind. The pastor and a doctor from Philadelphia and the merely curious had visited the sick girl and had come away muttering that God had surely taken her off, and maybe it was a mercy at that.

Gennie's dramatic reappearance, the tale of her survival and rescue, seared the town with excitement, just the thing to enliven a gray winter and a soggy spring. In the two taverns there was no cease of talk about the little indentured French girl, grown now to the legendary proportion of a Joan of Arc, wed to a lonely but cruel old man who was now seen with sweeping hindsight to have been sinfully perverted by lust all along. Thomas was Saint George, and the dragon was the devil who held Gennie's mind imprisoned in his mocking grip, while she waited for God's deliverance.

Would she ever be "right" again? Were her suffering and the death of her baby too painful for her ever to face again? The men debated in the taverns, the chambermaids in the kitchens of the prosperous, and the goodwives at prayer circle. Some instructed God to keep her mind veiled and let her live in the loving circle of her mother's new family the rest of her days. Others, of different courage and vigor, pulled God's ear and informed him she would be better off climbing out of her dream state: Life was meant to go on living!

The buzz followed Thomas wherever he went. He knew he could not live and work in Germantown. Perhaps he had failed Gennie. In the springtime of their love, glowing with the conviction that God had chosen them for each other, he had assured her that God had meant him to care for her always. But the months of Gennie's silence had unnerved him.

Twice, in the months before bringing her to the Ohio valley, he had had to leave her.

He had ridden north to Hartford, to present his dispatches to General Wolcott, to tender his resignation, and to collect his earnings and the money Wolcott had kept for him from fur sales.

Then he had ridden on to Boston to visit briefly with Peter Sparhawk and his family. Peter was engaged to a town girl, sparkling and full of wit, like he. Thomas elicited promises that the couple would someday visit him in the Ohio.

Returning to Germantown, he found Gennie as obedient as a docile child, her large eyes veiled of meaning, her expression lacking any depth beyond the moment. She had been taken in again by Zellaire, whom Marie Therese convinced that she could restore her daughter to health if anyone could, with God's help.

Seeing her, Thomas reached a decision. He awoke to it one morning and found it gave him peace.

"You can't take a woman away without wedding her!"

"How else can I take her?" Thomas paced the study where Parson Cullers had been trying for the last hour to convince him of the sin of his intended path.

"She loves me. She just can't say the vows yet, is all."

"Loves you? You are out of your head!"

"She came home with me, didn't she?"

"So would any white woman forced to live with savages."

"But—" Thomas thrust Gennie's journal at the pastor again.

"Yes, yes, I know she wrote that you loved her and she loved you. That was before she was wed, Thomas. Only divine Providence can possibly know what is in her mind now."

Thomas's chin jutted forward. "I do. God means for me to take care of Gennie, and by him I will!"

"Careful, Thomas."

"Good day, Pastor."

Wild words.

He had thought of them as he paused outside the Zellaire home. All the family was in the main living room as he entered. The happy scene would have struck a stranger as idyllic. Two of the children were carding yarn. Gennie would take a bit now and then and add it to the fluffy mass she was feeding onto the spinning wheel.

Henri and Marie Therese sat at the table, on which was spread a layer of dried beans. They were picking out the stones in preparation for planting the beans.

Gennie looked up with the detached smile she accorded everyone, then returned to her spinning. She looked well. Her cheeks bloomed. Her chestnut hair was washed and gleaming from scrupulous brushing, swept back and pinned in a loose bun at the nape.

After greetings, the children returned to their chattering, and Thomas slid on the bench beside Henri. "I am leaving for the Ohio tomorrow."

Henri nodded. They had been over this many times.

"By early summer I'll have a cabin up. Furniture."

"Thomas, don't you think—?"

"We agreed." His eyes bored into the distressed mother's eyes. "I will be back for Gennie in two months. Three at most."

Henri stopped sorting. "Now, Thomas," he said in a conciliatory tone, "what are you going to do with an invalid 'way out there?"

"She is not an invalid," he said quietly, flashing Gennie a reassuring smile, when he caught her gazing at him.

"You'll have plenty to do getting crops in, without worrying about someone as could wander off any time."

"We agreed that if Gennie is as she is now, when I have a place for her—and still willing—that you would let her go." Thomas heard the desperation edging into his voice. "Rosalind Hambleton is coming, too. I have already made an agreement with her. She is to stay with us until Gennie is well. Then I'm building her a cabin on her own piece of land. There's already English families living there. God knows they will appreciate having a midwife near."

"What will people—?"

"Hang fire what people think!" Thomas stomped to his feet and crossed to Gennie. He knelt gracefully beside the young woman.

"Gennie, heart, listen." Gennie's hands flew at their task until Thomas gently disengaged her fingers and held them loosely in his big hands. "I must leave you, just once more. It is too cold for you yet, where I am going. When I come back, you are coming home with me. Home. To our home. Do you understand, dear?"

Gennie smiled, waiting for whatever was supposed to happen next. Thomas's lips compressed, even as he gave her hands a gentle squeeze. He rose and faced the Zellaires. "Three months."

Thomas returned to the homeland of La Demoiselle. For days he rode through the land of the Miamis, seeking his farmland, finding it, finally, in a rich combination of prairie and woodlands, well watered by lakes and streams. It was from the edge of one of these lakes that he set off on foot one morning, accompanied by a host of braves and excited children, to pace the length of his land. Straight he walked, for thirty-six hours. La Demoiselle himself was there to greet him at the end and welcome him as a brother of the Miamis. The land was his. Thomas dropped to his knees and thanked God.

That had been six months ago. He had put crops in, with seed from the Miamis as well as from former neighbors in Germantown, and then his cabin.

He stared through the shimmery heat, watching Gennie as she stepped out the door of the cabin and walked sedately toward the vegetable garden. Rosalind's resonant voice drifted to him as she gave Gennie the occasional direction. A breeze came up and snapped the wet clothes on the line.

Suddenly tears sprang to Thomas's eyes. He did not know how much longer he could stand it. "God . . ." His voice broke. "I thought I was doing your will. I was so sure that all I had to do was get Gennie away from everything that had made her sick and unhappy, and everything would be all right. I was so sure that my love was enough. I love her so much it is tearing my gut out!"

He tasted salt in his mouth as he trudged doggedly down the row of corn. "It isn't enough to love, it isn't! Only you can make her well, Lord, I can't do it." Thomas sank to his knees and thumped his forehead with a fist.

The breeze rustled the corn, and Rosalind's melodious laughter mingled with the teasings of the boy. Thomas drove his hands into the warm soil. He felt the throbbing life between his fists. Yes. The Indians said the earth was alive, as much the Spirit Father's as the earthworm and the hawk. *Lord, you gave me this land. Give me back my Gennie! Let us raise a family that will bring honor to you and to this land . . . If you keep Gennie the way she is, that—that is all right, too.*

"I'll take care of her for you." Thomas took a deep breath and plunged on. He had feared this step, but now knew that he meant it and was ready to accept God's will. "And if you want me to marry someone else, well, that's your business, and I'll do the best I can to make you proud."

Clumsily, a little shamefaced for fear someone had seen or heard, Thomas got to his feet and beat at the crumbly earth clinging to his trousers. He swiped at his sweaty face with his bicep. His eyes felt gritty as he looked around. Rosalind was disappearing back toward the creek; he didn't see the boy; and Gennie was gone again.

Rosalind was doing a good job with her. Gennie seemed to need retraining, as if she had forgotten everything she had ever learned. Now, thanks to Rosalind, every afternoon she came of her own accord to weed and pull just enough vegetables for their supper and wash them. Thomas was afraid to trust her alone near the creek, so the boy would fetch a bucket of water for washing vegetables and carry it inside for her.

He watched now as Jean reappeared from the direction of the stream, weighted down with a heavy bucket of water, and disappeared into the cabin.

Inside the cabin, Gennie did not even glance at the boy as he lifted the water up to the table beside her vegetables and dashed out again. She was admiring the round, purple beets, with their luxuriantly dark, broad-leaved stems, which she had just pulled. Her fingers closed around a sun-warm carrot, and she held it aloft like a dagger before her eyes. Beautiful. It was a lovely color and so warm. She looked curiously at her hands.

She dropped the carrot, still examining her hands, and returned silently to the rocker Thomas had made for her. These hands in her lap. Her nails were white and perfect. Mama always inspected them each morning before she and Phillippe had lessons.

But these nails were broken and ingrained with dirt. She watched as the fingers rubbed each other. What a gritty feeling! A smile quivered in a corner of her mouth. She watched the hands as she rocked. A breeze entered the open door. It cooled her warm face. She gazed out into the dooryard. The hedge around the vegetable garden was gone. And the haymows. Too early for haymows.

Where was that Phillippe? And Mama. It was time to start the vegetables for their supper. Papa would be coming in from the fields soon. The smile trembled and vanished. No, there he was, it was all right.

Gennie watched as the figure rose again in the cornfield. Her blessed Savior felt very close to her now. She could feel the warmth of his love. She knew that whatever happened, whatever had happened, she lay in complete safety in his hands. Her lips moved in a child's grace she had sung before meals. She began to hum the tune.

Suddenly Gennie felt a buzzing in her ears. A strange excitement tingled in her veins. She could not bear to sit still. Her hands! How did they get so dirty? Mama would— No. The vegetables. The garden. Her breath came now in shallow, fearful gasps. She tiptoed toward the door. No! No hedge. Not Mama's garden. Of course not, it was her garden, hers and Thomas's and Rosalind's.

"Thomas!" Gennie screamed. "Thomas! Thomas Thomas Thomas!"

The man in the field stopped. He gazed in her direction. Suddenly he shouted, "Gennie!" and was running toward her.

They met at the edge of the field, in the fierce glare of the sun.

Gennie was sobbing, her hands outstretched. "My hands are dirty, from the garden. It's *my* garden, Thomas!" and Thomas shouting, "Praise God, Gennie, yes, yes, it's your garden!"

Then they were in each other's arms, Gennie clutching then pushing him back, cupping his face in her grimy fingers, the sweat of his face streaking to mud as his eyes bored into her, scared and disbelieving.

Tears sheeted down her face. Her eyes sparkled like a thousand suns, letting in the light, letting in memories—good and bad. Slowly Gennie closed her eyes and raised her face as if receiving a cleansing rain.

Thomas's lips murmured his thanks as he gathered her to him and bent his sunburned face to her lips.

·E·P·I·L·O·G·U·E·

 ennie Harmonie Amos Roebuck never became the strong-willed, independent woman her mother was, nor that her only granddaughter became. Sheltered by family and friends whom she loved and who loved her, she lived a sunny, productive life and bore many healthy children.

In later years peace with the Miamis collapsed, but the Roebuck lands were never violated. This was attributed to the gentle woman known to the Indians as Spirit-Who-Cries, who, as they all knew, was especially loved of the Great Spirit.

Gennie's journal was never written in again. After their marriage, Thomas laid it away in the saddleback chest in their bedroom, where it lay undisturbed until the day their irrepressible granddaughter whisked it outside and up in the hayloft. French she had learned as effortlessly as falling off a horse. Now she would discover why those who remembered her grandmother as a beautiful young woman said she looked just like her but . . . but that is another story.

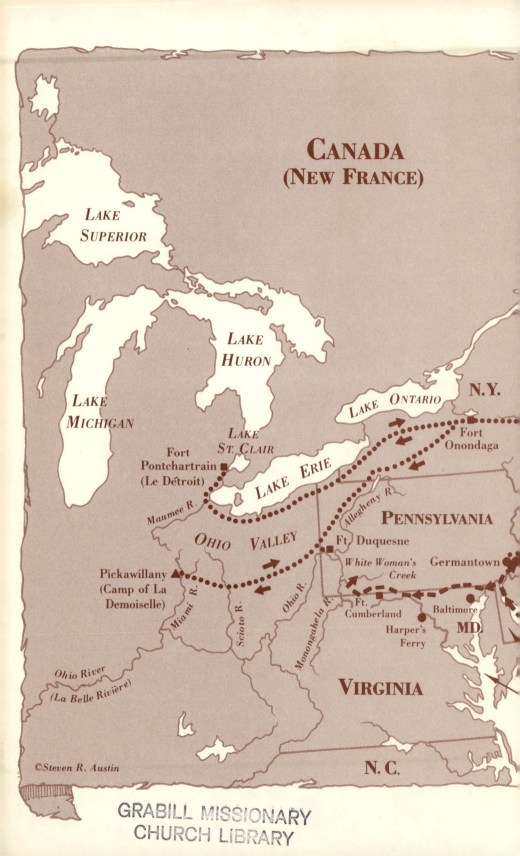

CANADA
(NEW FRANCE)

LAKE
SUPERIOR

LAKE
HURON

LAKE
MICHIGAN

LAKE
ST. CLAIR

LAKE ONTARIO

N.Y.

Fort
Onondaga

Fort
Pontchartrain
(Le Détroit)

LAKE ERIE

Maumee R.

Allegheny R.

PENNSYLVANIA

OHIO   VALLEY

Ft. Duquesne

White Woman's
Creek

Germantown

Pickawillany
(Camp of La
Demoiselle)

Miami R.

Scioto R.

Ohio R.

Monongahela R.

Ft.
Cumberland

Baltimore

MD

Harper's
Ferry

Ohio River
(La Belle Rivière)

VIRGINIA

©Steven R. Austin

N.C.